GOD BLESS MR. DEVIL

GOD BLESS MR. DEVIL

A NOVEL BY

ANDREW DAVIS

Moonscape Publishing

The characters—except for recognizable public figures—events, situations, and organizations in this story are purely fictitious, are used in a fictitious context, and have no basis whatsoever in the real world. Recognizable public figures represent, and are used only as, expressions of art in a fictitious context. This work is a manifestation of the writer's imagination, designed solely to entertain the reader. It is not intended to be a religious or spiritual directive, or to imply or sanction any religious or spiritual belief or assumption pertaining to the subject matter presented.

FIRST EDITION

Cover graphics by Kent Wildman

ISBN: 0-9675811-0-9

Library of Congress Card Number: 99-067880

2000 01 02 03 04 05 ♲ 10 9 8 7 6 5 4 3 2 1

Moonscape Publishing, 2017 Shawnee Lane, Greenbrier, TN 37073

This book is dedicated to the loving memory of Karen Michelle Hite, 1975-1992. If there ever was an angel who could lead the Devil to love, it would be you, sweetheart.

ACKNOWLEDGMENTS

I owe sincere and eternal thanks to Dr. Joe Filippo who, so long ago, encouraged me to write, and to Noel Kirby-Smith, whose profound and lasting influence is on every page I have ever written. I love you, John. Thank you, Gerry, for asking a brilliant question and for your generous support. To Janet, for her timely insight. Jimmy, I appreciate you. Special thanks to Sarah, who read it first and took it apart so I could rebuild it. Frances, you made it a better book. Phyllis, I'm so fortunate to have you in my corner. Thank you, Bob, for saying all the right things at exactly the right time. Special thanks to Kent Wildman for his most gracious and devilish graphic artistry. Thanks to Travis and Jeffry for all their help and wisdom. Special thanks to Maryglenn at Dowling Press for her unconditional kindness and guidance. Penelope, thank you so much for your relentless support and empowerment, especially when the tunnel was a dark and lonely place. And from the depths of my soul, I thank my loving wife, Susan, whose brilliant suggestions, tireless input and editing, patience, faith, and endless love made all the difference.

1

Sunday, December 1

Satan emerged from his bedroom with a boyish anticipation on his ragged face and scurried into the main chamber of his lair in Hell.

A trail of popcorn erupted from a brown bag pinned between his arm and his chest while he hurriedly mopped his face and hair with a towel. He flung the towel aside, flopped into his favorite chair in the middle of the room and snapped his fingers. A giant television monitor embedded in the far wall hissed to life.

Good evening from the Global News Group. I'm Richard Atworthy in Washington.

"All right! Just in time," Satan declared. He

reached into a big red plastic cooler on the floor next to his recliner and pulled out an icy long-neck beer. "What's happenin', Richard? Give it to me, baby!" He twisted the top off the beer and carelessly hurled it over his shoulder.

Fighting between Chinese government forces and the so-called "Democratic Freedom Fighters" continues to rage out of control at this hour in two major provinces of that country. Over five hundred people, mostly civilians, are known dead in Beijing alone, and fighting is reported outside Shenyang, a major industrial city to the northeast of Beijing. Also, India has been warned to avoid considering DFF activity in the western provinces as an "opportunity"—so the Chinese government put it. Most authorities agree there appears to be no solution in sight outside a major retaliation by the Chinese military.

In another hot spot, over two hundred thousand Chinese troops are reported massed along their border with North Korea in response to the recent flare-up between North and South Korea. The U.S. Secretary of State and NATO have been notified that the Chinese military is at full alert and will remain so indefinitely.

"Yeah! That's what we want! What a mess!" Satan burst out laughing at the good news, thrust the beer toward the screen, and slapped his knee with approval.

Also in tonight's news, we have reports that an unknown virus is responsible for an unprecedented and deadly viral outbreak in Ghana. If it cannot be contained and escapes the borders of that African country, it could possibly threaten the world. No one knows what it is, where it came from, or how to combat it. We take you to—

Church bells in the bell tower at the Faith Community Church in Atlanta, Georgia rang in the joy of the Christmas season on this beautiful Sunday morning. God's world was a crystal wonderland, the air pristine, crisp, and silent in the wake of an early winter storm and seven inches of snow. The little whitewashed stone church, Gothic in appearance with its steep towers, roof, and multitude of stained glass windows, shot into a sapphire blue sky that draped the frozen world. Cottony cumulous clouds drifted lazily overhead. A radiant sun had squeezed its way above the horizon and now poured its bronze rays through the tapestry of ancient white oaks that greeted the parishioners as they gathered into a colorful fan at the church steps. God's flowers, seeking The Light, Reverend Fred Frey thought. God bless them all.

Humble, slight and slump-shouldered, the Reverend Fred Frey was a walking stick of a man with a tuft of gray hair that resembled a badger sunning itself on a rock. His chest curled inward from a lifetime of leaning toward his congregation when he shook their hands. Thick, dark-rimmed glasses magnified his eyes. The imposing Bible he carried dominated his appearance in the way a lighthouse beacon dominates its tower. Chosen by Him at an early age, Reverend Frey saw himself as God's messenger, and often compared himself to that lighthouse. He was "God's tower, standing on the rocky, treacherous shores of Evil," and his Bible was "God's beacon in the night that warned all who approached." He preached against Satan with such vehemence that one elderly lady in the church swore that the floor under her feet shook whenever he was in the pulpit.

"Good morning, Bill," the Reverend said to the man before him. "A blessed Advent season to you and your lovely family. Good morning, Joan. And look at these fine children," he said, smiling down at the twin girls who stood in their parents' shadows. He reached for their hands. "How are my little darlings this morning?"

"Fine, Mr. Frey," they said in unison.

"Well good, good. God bless you!

"And you, John, good morning. I feel like saying Merry Christmas already!

"Morning, Tom, Millie," he said, waving to a couple beyond the line. No one would enter God's church without recognition. "Is it not a beautiful day in God's world? We are so blessed!

"*Good* morning. *Good* morning. Merry Christmas!

"Good morning, Paul, and how are you?"

"Fine Reverend," the man said.

"Good, good. God bless you, Rachael.

"And what about you, Katie darling," he said to the little girl holding her mother's hand. He squatted down. "Look how lovely you are! How's my beautiful little angel this morning?" he said with a bright smile.

At the tender age of eight, Katie Hart had her mother's European cheekbones and golden hair, and her eyes were as blue as the heavens themselves. She wore a blue dress that intensified the blue in her eyes, and two delicate lace bows in her hair separated it into ponytails on either side. She was his favorite child, good-natured, intensely perceptive, intelligent, and she even paid attention to his sermons.

"Fine, Reverend Frey. How are you today?" Katie replied with the demeanor and grace of a princess.

"Fine, fine, my sweet. God bless you."

"What's the lesson today, Reverend Frey?"

"Katie!" the mother said with embarrassed surprise. "Forgive her, Reverend. She wants to know *everything*."

"Why, of course she does," the preacher said.

He shot a disarming smile at Katie. "Today's lesson is about prayer, angel; the power of prayer. Do you say your prayers at night?"

"Yes, sir."

"Well good, good. God loves you, my sweet."

Satan stuffed popcorn into his mouth.

...bloody civil war across the Sudan and Ethiopian borders is raging out of control, and the United Nations and the United States have been called upon to pressure the warring factions into backing off. Ravaged by drought and plagued by political tensions created when Libya began funneling arms and money to militant rebels inside Sudan, the area has boiled into a hot spot.

In a statement to the world press this morning, Egyptian authorities said that any action directed toward Egyptian borders by hostile factions will be considered a direct military threat by Libya, and will result in, as the source put it, "Libyan genocide."

A ghoulish laugh rose from the tattered recliner and reverberated off the stone walls of Satan's lair. "I got 'em confused now! Look at 'em runnin' for cover!"

...worst winter storms in decades continue to plague the southeast. Temperatures have been in the low teens for a week, deep snow blankets

most of the southern states, including northern Florida, and there seems to be no relief from the cold in sight until after the Christmas Season. We take you to...

"Satan's puttin' in a lot of *overtime*!"

Reverend Frey flung his head back in defiance and repeated the phrase to make sure the Devil heard him. "Satan's puttin' in a lot of overtime, folks!"

He broke away from the lectern, his opened Bible recklessly held high in one hand and flung about as he paced the pulpit. "The most violent and unusual global weather systems in history are destroying crops and lives and driving food prices to all-time record highs. Pushed beyond her limits, Mother Earth is in rebellion! She's had enough! We got people everywhere—little children—starving to death!

"We have an unknown and deadly virus on the loose in Africa that threatens to spread throughout the world and kill millions if the modern medicine of mankind can't find a way to stop it.

"Social and moral decay is rampant in the streets of a world gone straight to Hell.

"We got w*ars* all over the world!"

His fist came crashing down on the lectern.

"We've got over two hundred *thousand*

American troops on red alert in South Korea on this very day, young lives about to be put to the sword to satisfy Satan's insatiable taste and appetite for human souls! Our world is *enshrouded* in a dark veil of evil that blocks out The Light, and Satan is the cause of it all!" he snarled, an accusing finger shooting toward his bleak audience.

He dropped his Bible on the lectern, took a breath and glanced down at precious little Katie Hart. God help her, he thought. She would grow up in a world held in Satan's grip, a world torn and twisted by Evil. Never before had he seen such tribulation and human suffering as in the last few weeks.

The lone wail of a crying child echoed in the stifling silence that followed the Reverend's proclamation. As if ordained, sunlight suddenly streamed in through the stained glass windows, filling the church with a kaleidoscope of color. It was his cue to lighten up and slow the pace. He knew that, because the same child always cried.

"But God has the answer," he said with a calm smile, slowly placing his hands on the rim of the lectern, looking out across his congregation with hope in his eyes. "Jesus says in Matthew 5:44, 'But I tell you: Love your enemies and *pray* for those who persecute you, that you may be sons of your Father in Heaven,' " he said quickly.

"Prayer!"

The fist hit the lectern again.

"Prayer...is the answer. Webster's dictionary tells us that prayer is 'a humble and sincere request to *God*,' but I say to you that prayer is a tool, *created* by God, that allows our Creator to bring love into our lives and pass it on to others. It exists outside of us, and resides wholly within God Himself. Prayer is God's Internet, folks, and love is God's World Wide Web. We must *log on* and seek God's deliverance from Evil.

"We must pray...for our world.... We must come unto God as the little children do," he smiled down at Katie Hart, his hand going out to her, "and pray for deliverance from Satan's grasp."

He placed his hands in a position of prayer. "As we go our separate ways in God's light this morning, I challenge each and every one of you to place a world leader, a government body, one of our enemies, someone who desperately needs God's help and guidance on your prayer list today. Their burden is heavy, and their path is steep.

"Now, you might say, but Reverend Frey, how is it possible that my insignificant little prayers can be heard above the roar of worldwide evil?" He thumbed the pages of his Bible. "Jesus tells us, 'I tell you the truth, if anyone says to this mountain, Go, throw yourself into the sea, and does not doubt in his heart but believes that what he says will happen, it will be done for him. Therefore I tell you, whatever you ask for in prayer, believe that you have received it, and it will be yours.' Through prayer and love we will *defeat* Satan and build a better world for our children."

Dabbing with a white handkerchief at the residue of sweat that lingered on his forehead, Reverend Frey stood in the foyer under the arched double doorway of his church and shook the hands of his congregation as they filed out. "Merry Christmas and God bless you...yes, God bless you and Merry Christmas. God bless you, Jim; y'all come back now."

Katie Hart stopped in front of the preacher, her little Bible held in her left hand. "Reverend Frey, why doesn't anyone pray for the Devil?"

"My goodness, Katie Hart!" her mother said.

The preacher covered the implied apology with a smile and squatted in front of Katie. "Well, because it wouldn't do any good. You see, the Devil is one of several angels who got into trouble in Heaven, and God sent them to live in Hell where they have to stay until Judgement Day."

"Can the Devil be saved, like us?" she asked.

"Well, no," he said. "That's why God sent him and the other angels away."

"Oh. I see...." She frowned. "Why can't he be saved?"

"Well, because God *wants* it that way," the Reverend said. "It's God's will, angel."

Katie's little face lit up. "Thank you, Reverend Frey," she said, and walked out into the sunlight. She knew exactly what she had to do.

2

The Devil lay sprawled in his old tortured chair, wrapped in a black bathrobe millions of years old, now speckled with popcorn debris. His feet, barely hidden by the remnants of the only pair of house shoes he'd ever owned, were flopped up on the coffee table before him. His doctors had told him he shouldn't sit like that because it didn't help the circulation problem in his legs. Seemed like they complained about everything he did nowadays. His only real pleasure in life was a torpedo-shaped Havana cigar jutting from his teeth. It wasn't lit. The same doctors who whined about the only position that he found immensely comfortable also had told him that smoke was killing him. Of course smoke was killing him. Smoke was an occupational hazard in this place.

He didn't look much like the traditional Devil that everybody got all wound up about. All that stuff about horns and a pointed tail was idiocy, an attempt by the do-gooders in the world to keep humans under the repressive thumb of fear. In reality, he had a receding hairline where horns should have been, his vanishing hair now a ghost of its former existence. And his butt—where the tail should have been—was rather flat. The local joke was that God had flattened it when he "booted the Old Man's ass out of Heaven."

Well, that was all right. He might be the "Old Man" with a flat ass, but he was still the Devil and he was still in charge, because here he sat, watching the world come apart on GNG, and enjoying every minute of it.

The chamber itself was sparse and bleak, only the bare necessities of life in Hell were present. What did someone with most of the known universe in his grasp need?

The entire space was a dismal, gray, stone virtual reality carved into the face of time, its surface cracked and twisted by torturous heat. There were no windows, only a curved wall of virtual glass, extending the breadth of the chamber—the Overlook into the flickering inferno of Hell. He had expanded this "window onto Hell" into his main control room to remind his cronies how fortunate they were. Except for Benny, no one who had ever served in the control room had gone to the Overlook more than once. The glass was a one-way street. Souls passed through it, but never returned. Benny often stood in front of it, staring for hours.

An ornately carved stone bar separated the main chamber from the dining area. The gargoyle faces of tortured souls decorated its oppressive facade. A number of faceted crystal decanters filled with fine whiskey, all dulled by the dust of time, lined the shelves and stood sentry over his past. Debilitating headaches had caused him to give that up. The bar did little more now than serve as a reminder of the glory days, days when the world was young and filled with the challenge of conquest.

A black marble dining table and matching chairs, an imposing island of stone, rose out of the floor to the left of the living area. Demons emerged from within its intricately engraved superstructure and thick edges. It was never used.

A Roman numeral clock, encircled by tormented griffin figures but devoid of hands, hung on the wall opposite the Overlook—time didn't matter down here. In the main chamber, a beat-up wrought-iron coffee table supported a gold inlaid humidor filled with fresh Havana cigars, an ongoing gesture of good faith from the dictator in Cuba.

The other end, close to the recliner, held a large red recessed button. Entombed in a thick mesh of dingy cobwebs, an ancient red telephone, the hot line to God, occupied the center of the table. He had it installed because he thought that someday, maybe someday, God would call. God never called, and the phone had never been used.

In a remote corner where the wall joined the Overlook, a black chest held together by bold, fiendish fittings of pure gold hunkered in the shadows. In the purest of microscopic gold threads that were formed in The Beginning, an elaborate pictorial etching of the story of Creation covered its surface. So fine were they in detail, their meaning would escape the human eye. Nowadays, without his glasses, the images even eluded Satan's sight. Were it not for the fact that they were burned into his memory, he feared they would someday be lost forever.

The small chest held the only personal belonging he had managed to escape with when God exiled him: his personal diary, slipped out under the protection of his power. Recorded on its pages were the early days of his childhood in Heaven, how he came to sit at the left hand of God, and in rebellious detail, written in red after the trouble started, the story of his descent into disillusionment and his eventual expulsion from Heaven.

He rarely read the diary now, seldom ever

held it in his hands. Only when times were good, like now, when he felt powerful enough to withstand the impact of its cherished memories, did he dare touch it, read it. Tonight it lay on the coffee table just beyond his reach. Once the hallmark of a proud young warrior who challenged the status quo, it was now a symbol of pain and regret that haunted the dreams of an exhausted old angel.

The thing that occupied his time now was what had come to be known as "The Wall." A virtual computer network, its several monitors and control consoles covered one whole side of the chamber from ceiling to floor perpendicular to the Overlook, and served as his window onto the universe. Every operation he had underway, including those in the main control room and all his personal endeavors, could be tracked from this one room. The entire universe was laid out before him.

Snapping his fingers, he killed GNG and brought his fist down on the red button built into the coffee table. He flopped back in the chair and bellowed a mocking laugh as an image of the chaos in the control center formed in his head. It was the Pavlov dogs thing—amazing how that worked—and he loved it. He gave it another 10 seconds, enough time for the crew to get into an uproar, then shouted, "Get in here, Benny!"

Over the intercom, the gut-wrenching scream of a soul in pain shattered the hum of computer background noise in Hell's main control center and set off a wild frenzy of system checks and cross-references. The scream was a new twist on an eternal alarm system that left the crew no doubt as to where they were.

"Here he comes!" Benny lunged from his console to his section controller and leaned over his shoulder. "Let's go. All red sectors up. He'll want the red sectors."

"I got 'em," the boy at the console assured him.

"All right! Red sectors online! Get it done, people!" Benny shouted over the top of the cubicle.

Get in here, Benny! the Devil's voice boomed over the speakers.

The Kid slapped his console and shoved away from the screen. "Why does he always do that? I thought that alarm system was for emergencies."

Benny grinned down at him sarcastically. "Because this is Hell," he said. Concern replaced the smile. "Something's wrong or he wouldn't want to see me. Don't take any chances. Keep those red sectors running until I get back in here." He patted his young friend on the back. "You're good, Kid."

The Kid, a computer genius, was the very genius who had busted the Pentagon's mainframe just three years ago and brought down NORAD a week later. He was young, but he knew how to take orders, and he did good work, so Benny had put him in charge of the board when he lost his main controller to the Overlook.

The Kid's timing had been perfect. Had he not been killed when he was, by a mysterious bus wreck on his way to prison, he might have gone to the Lake of Fire. Stupid fools. The government could have used him if they'd kept him alive. By wiping him out, they had placed him in a position where he could do damage beyond their wildest dreams.

"Hey." The boy grabbed Benny's arm and pulled his boss down. "What's it like in there?" he whispered. "Is it like this?" He gestured at the sweat running down his body.

The control room was a hellish steam bath of heat and humidity in a rat's maze of cramped stone cubicles lit by blue imaging screens. Benny's last main console controller had complained about the heat—just a few days ago. Wrong. Now, a perpetual, steaming moisture covered everything: walls, floor, consoles, bodies, the Overlook glass. The incessant, refracted orange flicker of Hell's fire through the Overlook served as a ghoulish, dripping reminder of what lay beyond the miserable comfort of the control room.

Benny shook his head pitifully. "You don't want to know, Kid. Trust me."

"Oh, yes!" the Kid said quickly, tightening his grip. "I do. I dream about it at night."

Benny nodded. "All right," he said. He lowered himself to one knee and rested his arm on the boy's shoulder. "First of all," he did an obvious scan of the area to make sure no one was listening before he leaned close to the boy's ear and said, "it's *air*-conditioned."

The Kid groaned.

"Yeah," Benny said, caught up in his impromptu fantasy. "And he keeps an ice chest filled with *cold beer* next to his chair." He muzzled the boy's mouth with a hand to muffle the cries of agony. "It's so cold," Benny said with unrestrained passion, holding up the other hand to show the imaginary scars, "it'll burn your hand," he whispered, licking his lips. "And there's always three or four of the most beautiful women you've ever seen in there, walking around topless in French-cut, silk-lace panties."

The Kid squeezed his eyes closed. Tears flowed down across Benny's hand and dripped onto the keyboard.

"See," Benny said with another smile and a pat on the back. "I told you you didn't want to know."

Get in here, Benny!

"Yes sir!"

He raced for the Devil's lair.

Benny entered the chamber and stopped just inside the door. He was average height, lean and muscular, his features bold and chiseled, in excellent shape when he was killed. A highly successful criminal defense trial lawyer in his past life, he had lived in the gym and in court. Yet, it was all he could do to breathe, the air so hot he could hear his lungs sizzling inside his head.

Satan's main operations screen displayed The Weather Channel's satellite graphic of North America, the volume down. The Devil lounged in the recliner with that gigantic cigar pinched between his teeth, his hand wrapped around a longneck beer that rested on top of the big red cooler next to the chair. Benny tried with all his strength, even the strength Satan had issued him, but he could not take his eyes off that sweating beer.

Satan snapped his fingers and The Weather Channel went away. "Benny! Benny, my boy!" Satan boomed. "Come in, come in!" the beer waving him into the room, moisture droplets flying from its surface like buckets of ice water.

Benny moved cautiously toward the coffee table and stood semi-rigid in the stifling heat. Satan's diary lay next to the red phone—a good sign.

With a bit of effort, the Devil climbed out of the chair using one knee as a prop and made his way around the coffee table, beer in hand. The Old Man's arthritis was flaring up again. He always drank when that happened, and in this condition, he'd be as unpredictable as a Kodiak bear—*not* a good sign.

"Benny, my boy, we're doin' some good work," Satan declared, beginning to straighten up. "We got the world in an uproar, and everything's goin' our way. That civil war in China is one of the finest pieces of work I've ever seen," he said. "The military of *every nation in the world* is on red alert. Uprisings have been reported all the way from Beijing to the Himalayas. Cities burnin' out of control, the proletariat infected with rage, soldiers gunnin' down women and children in the streets." The Devil slapped Benny on the back so hard he almost quit breathing. "Damn fine piece of work if I've ever seen it.

"And you did a fine job of gettin' those idiots in Washington off Castro's back. Exposin' that assassination plot against him to the media blew the whole thing open."

"Thank you, sir. I know how important that is to you," Benny plugged. "The media can be a powerful tool. I often used it to create chaos in the courts."

"Yeah, you were a brilliant attorney, and I certainly don't need any trouble in Cuba." He pointed his cigar at the lawyer. "The man ain't much on social finesse, but he makes a fine cigar.

"Now, I told Mubundi to make a move in the

Sudan, so we gotta keep an eye on that. You with me?"

"Yes, sir. You think he'll do it?"

"Yeah, he'll do it," Satan assured him. "He'll do whatever I say. If there ever was a man possessed, he is.

"I warned Chuwang, our rebel leader in China, about them tryin' to set him up with that meeting. You trackin' that?"

"Yes, sir," Benny declared.

"I got to the North Korean delegation this mornin'. As long as I can keep the pressure on them there won't be any meetings with South Korea.

"And I'm gonna do all the follow-up on the virus in Africa. Make it my personal project. I'm workin' on two people who'll spread it to North America and Asia by the end of the month." He pursed his lips and shook his finger to make a point. "You know, if I pull this off, I can wipe out half the world's population before they stop it." A cruel laugh. "What a great Christmas present!"

Benny chuckled along. "Yes, sir."

Satan made his way to the Overlook and now faced the glass. "It's been a hard six weeks, but we're on a roll." He turned. "You and the boys have done a good job. So, here's what we're gonna do." He flung his hand at Benny. "*Christmas* is comin'," he teased. "I want you to take some time off. Put the B-team in on a standby watch, and you and the rest of the guys kick back for a while."

The Devil stood there with a Cheshire cat grin surrounding the cigar sticking out of his face. "Uh, do you feel all right, sir?" Benny queried tactfully.

Satan burst into a laugh. "'Course I feel all right, boy." He took Benny's arm and led him toward the door. "It's just that these last few weeks have been hard on all of us, and I haven't slept in days. I'm gonna take a break and get some rest. You and the boys cool it for a while. I'll check in with you before I turn in."

Benny exited the Devil's lair wiping sweat from his face and approached his controller. There would be no break tonight, no matter what the boss said. After weeks of hard work and the Old Man in such a good mood, he'd take no chances on something going wrong at this point.

"If it's air-conditioned in there, why do you always come out in a sweat?" the Kid said.

Benny glared down at him. "I vaguely remember mentioning beautiful women in French panties the last time I saw you." He flicked a hand at his master controller's screen. "Punch up the status reports for all sectors."

The Kid hit the keys. "What's up?"

"Hopefully nothing," Benny said, his attention riveted to the screen. "The Old Man just did the first good thing I've ever seen him do. All right, run a continuity brief on all sectors, set up an auto-scan on any that have a stability factor of ninety percent or better, and I want secondary alert scanners in place."

"Whoa, what gives?"

"The Old Man's got the Christmas spirit," Benny said. "I want to make sure he keeps it as long as possible. Everyone in auto-scan status can relax until further notice, as long as they don't leave their stations. That includes you. Place all the other consoles under Priority Remote Interface and route them to my cubicle. Those people will have one hour to rest before they go back online." He straightened up and wiped his face. "The Old Man's exhausted, and he's gonna sleep tonight."

"All right!"

"Yeah, well you know how he is," Benny warned. "We're not taking any chances. When you're at the top the only place to go is down. You keep those secondary scanners running as long as we're in auto-scan status. If something goes wrong now, all hell'll break loose."

Four hours later, Satan lingered in front of the control screens embedded in The Wall in his lair. Shrouded in the old housecoat, the remains of a beer dangling from one hand, his diary now in the other, he watched the various screens flicker with universal activity. The main ninety-six-inch screen dominated The Wall; five other thirty-inch monitors were mounted in a row below it. "I'll pay for this in the mornin'," he admitted, "but sometimes you just gotta let business go for a while." He cocked an eye at Benny. "You know how long it's been since I've had a vacation?"

Benny let his shoulders relax a little. The Old Man was pretty much under the influence and hopefully on his way to a peaceful night. "You haven't taken one since I've been here, sir."

"Yeah!" Satan blurted, "I haven't had one since *I've* been here." He issued a tired sigh. "And I've been here a long time," he said with great remorse to some distant ear.

Satan swung the beer bottle toward the red phone on his coffee table. "It's times like this I wanna get on that phone with God and try to call a truce for just one night. Sleep that deathly sleep I used to enjoy when I was a child," he said, swaying like a giant tree in a subtle wind. "'Course I've never made the call. God ain't got much of a sense of humor about that kind of thing." He snapped his fingers and the main control screen changed channels. "God ain't got a sense of humor about *anything*," he huffed.

"If he did, I'd let him in on this." He held up the diary and showed it to Benny. "Everything anybody ever wanted to know about God, Heaven, Hell, the nature of Creation and Time...me, is recorded in the pages of this diary. I wrote down everything. God doesn't even know about it, and if I told him about it, he'd only try to use it against me." He shook his head and carefully laid the diary on the coffee table. "What a pity."

A buffalo herd materialized on the main screen before his watery eyes. There they were, hundreds of them, scattered in the New Mexico desert, their heads down, magnificent grunting sculptures carved from the barren landscape by a white-hot full moon, their frosted backs a sparkling sea of desert whitecaps.

"See that?" The beer went up in a salute. "What do you think that is?" Satan asked. He took a drink.

Benny's eyes repeatedly flashed from the screen to Satan in an attempt to pick up on the Old Man's train of thought. "Uh, sir, I'd say that's a...herd of buffalo."

"*Ted Turner's* buffalo."

"Yes, sir. Ted Turner's buffalo," Benny agreed.

Satan dawdled for the longest time, his

thoughts suspended between the tranquility of their world and the chaos of his. “Look at you guys,” he said in a forlorn tone. “Got Ted Turner feedin’ you, coyotes singin’ you to sleep at night, nothin’ to do but eat and sleep, maybe...stampede every now and then.” He chuckled mischievously before his expression grew sour. “What a life,” he said painfully, waving the beer bottle around in a gesture of acknowledgement. “You even got horns.”

He harrumphed. “It ain’t what it used to be,” he said. “Back in the good old days when people were ignorant and we had the Romans, the Dark Ages, the witch hunts, when war and death were the only practical methods of transferring power—that’s when it was *jumpin’*,” he said, throwing an uppercut to an invisible stomach.

“But don’t get me wrong,” he said in defense of himself, a finger coming up. “I did some good work back in the forties, fifties, Viet Nam, all that. We’re doin’ okay. At least these days we got television and the Internet workin’ for us. It’s just that after you’ve burned a few billion souls it loses its flair. Now it seems like the only justification for burnin’ *one* is to burn another one.”

He wearily shook his head. “What an irony,” he said. “Because of my own initiative, I’ve reduced myself to the status of babysitter for a conquered world with nothin’ to do now but watch it burn. Sometimes I just wanna cut it all loose.

You know, build a winter home in New Mexico, slide down an endless hill in a fresh snow...on my belly...my arms stuck out in front of me," he did that, "my feet kickin' up a frosty spray behind me, like those downhill skiers do."

He gripped the neck of the beer and held it in front of him. "But it's kind of like...havin' some evil beast by the neck," he said. "Long as you hold on, you're all right. You just can't let go." He relaxed his grip on the bottle. "And since I don't know how to do anything else, I can't let go.... Hey, I know," he said with sudden insight. "Maybe I could do those credit card commercials, where nobody knows the guy when he travels."

Benny played along with a chuckle. "You serve an important role, sir," he offered. "Why, where would the duality of Good and Evil be without you? We wouldn't need cops, prisons, armies, locks, homeless shelters, food banks, even religion. Millions of people would be out of work. And Evil is an extremely important population control mechanism. Without it, the earth would be overrun with people. And it drives the world's economies," Benny continued. "Evil generates technology. Think about all the good ideas and products that have been generated by crime and wars. Without Evil, we'd all be living in mud huts. Evil is cool, sir...and so are you...."

"Yeah," Satan countered with a laugh. "I

never thought about it like that." He spread his arms. "I guess we're all doin' God's work down here."

"Yes, sir. I think you can say that, sir," Benny chirped.

Satan returned his attention to the screen for a moment, wavering slightly, the only sound that of the grunting buffalo, grazing in quiet solitude. Muted puffs of steam rose from their nostrils like wisps of smoke from the smoldering aftermath of a forest fire. "I've always wanted horns," he said solemnly.

"Yes, sir. I know," Benny acknowledged sadly.

Satan nodded, almost to himself and flicked his hand at Benny. "Go get some rest."

"Thank you, sir."

Satan watched his lawyer go. His gaze drifted back to the screen, to the stars—those ancient cosmic fireflies that lit up the universe, to the cottonwoods that hung from the night sky like giant parachutes...to the buffalo.

He grunted.

The buffalo seemed to answer his call.

Amused with the accuracy of his initial imitation, he did it again...and again, chuckling to himself. He breathed on one end of his cigar and watched it flare and glow red. He studied the screen again then stuck the cigar back into his mouth and slumped over and arched his back, using his fingers to form imaginary horns on his head. "Come on you guys, let's have a little fun," he said. "Let's *stampede*."

With smoke puffing out of his nose and mouth, Satan lumbered around the room bellowing thunder noises and charging through an imaginary desert night.

3

When Rachael Hart entered the room, Katie was sitting in bed with her mother's Bible in her lap and Freebie lying beside her. She also had her school writing notebook unfolded on the bed, its pages covered with scribbling, and her dictionary lying next to it.

"Oh, hi, Mom."

"Hi, sweetheart, what on earth are you doing? You're supposed to be asleep."

Katie shrugged. "I know," she said, yawned, "but I wanted to know some things about God, so I looked up His name, just like you do sometimes. I used your Bible because it has more words in the back than mine does."

"Well, that's okay," her mother said, collecting the results of Katie's work and laying it aside, "but we need to finish this tomorrow; it's way past your bedtime." Her mother tucked a fuzzy brown Teddy bear under her daughter's arm and cuddled the covers up under her neck.

Freebie lay on the bed next to Katie, his little body alongside hers. Her father had named the dog when he rescued him from the gas chamber at the pound. "He's a fifty-seven if there ever was one," the keeper had said, a crude mix—so they told him—between "a short hair and a long hair." The resulting genetic mutation was a small, wiry dog with an anteater snout and spiky brownish hair tipped with black. Regardless of his looks, he was Katie's loyal companion, and she loved him beyond human understanding.

"There you go," her mother said. "Now, did you add someone to your prayer list?"

"Yes, I did."

Her mother smiled approvingly. "Good," she said. "Then, let's say a prayer and we're off to bed."

Katie appeared thoughtful for a moment and said, "Mom, I've been wondering why no one prays for the Devil."

Her mother took a deep breath and weighed the statement. "Well, it's like Reverend Frey told you. A long time ago when the Devil got into trouble in Heaven, God sent him to live in Hell until Judgement Day. So it won't do any good to pray for him."

Katie immediately sat up in bed, her eyes now alert and filled with interest. "I've been thinking about that," she said. "In Matthew, chapter nineteen, verse twenty-six, Jesus says that God can do whatever he wants. It also says that in Luke. So that means that God can change his mind."

Rachael Hart's eyes widened. "You found all that?"

"Yes," Katie said with delight. "I looked in the back, like you've told me to do with other books, found God's name, and looked in the front where all the books of the Bible are listed, and then looked up the numbers and read what Jesus said."

"Why, that's wonderful! I'm so proud of you.... And to answer your question, yes, I suppose God can change his mind if he wants to, but he's not likely to do that."

"But it's possible," Katie said.

"Yes...I'd say it's...*possible*."

"Then God can give the Devil another chance if he wants to," Katie said with satisfaction. "So we should have faith that he will do that. I looked up faith, too. I think it means to believe that something will happen. Jesus told the blind man he got back his sight because he had faith. And the Bible says that faith won't work without deeds. So then

I looked up deeds in my dictionary, and those are things we do, so that means we should have faith and *do* things. Reverend Frey even told us that today. He said—I wrote it down," she said, reaching for and digging through her notes. "Whatever you ask for in prayer, believe that you have received it, and it will be yours. So," she summarized, "we should pray for the Devil, and we should believe that God will give him another chance."

"My goodness, you've been busy."

"It was hard," Katie said. "Sometimes I didn't know what the words meant, but I got most of it. The important thing is that we should pray for the Devil."

Her mother nodded affirmation to the apparent logic. "Of course the Devil would have to *want* to be saved, and I don't think he does."

"Which is why we should pray for him," Katie said enthusiastically. "If we all pray for him, maybe he'll change his mind, and God will change *His* mind, the Devil will be saved, and all the bad things in the world will stop happening."

Rachael Hart stared into her daughter's penetrating little eyes, the monumental simplicity and unparalleled implications of the child's argument blocking any attempt to explain it away. She smiled and kissed Katie on her forehead. "Perhaps," she said. "Now, enough about the Devil. We have to take Freebie to the Vet's office early tomorrow, and you need to be thinking about the Christmas play and the rehearsal and all the fun things that Santa Claus will bring you in a few days."

Katie frowned. "Mom, is Freebie going to be all right?"

Rachael smiled. "Yes, darling. They're just going to take a look at that knot on his leg to see if it needs to be removed."

"Good," Katie said. "And I've already memorized my lines for the play."

Rachael gave her a mischievous look. "You could have gotten the part of Mary if you'd wanted it," she said.

"I know," Katie admitted. She shrugged. "But each of the other girls really wanted to be Mary, too." A faint smile. "So I just thought I'd be an angel."

Her mother grabbed her in a hug. "Oh, I know, darling, and I love you so much for being *my* angel."

"Besides," Katie said when her mother released her. "I think being an angel is cool—the *Devil* is an angel."

Rachael Hart wiped a tear from her eye. "I know that, too," she said. "Now let's say a prayer and off you go."

Katie wiggled her way under the covers. Freebie lay with his needle nose on his paws. With her Teddy bear in her arms, Katie placed her hands together, closed her eyes, and began to pray. "Dear God. God bless Mom and Dad. God bless Teddy and Freebie. God bless the food we eat and the friends we keep. God bless all the bad people in the world...and God bless the Devil."

The nightmare drove Satan bolt upright in bed. Gasping for breath, his face soaked in sweat, his fist came down hard on the red button imbedded in his nightstand.

The deafening scream shattered the quiet hum of computer white noise in Hell's main control center.

Chaos exploded like a back draft. Feet kicked the bottoms of consoles. Bodies jerked erect. Hands flew to keyboards, frantically searching for the keys that would get their sector online before the whoosh of the door to Satan's lair signaled his arrival on the floor.

"ASS initiate!" Benny yelled. He stabbed the Automated Sector Search button on his console.

The Devil burst from his chamber like a mad bull. The heavy door to his crypt slammed against the wall.

"What was it!" he yelled, storming into the

room. "What the hell was that? I want answers!"

Gone was the old man Benny had seen just six hours earlier. He was still in the bathrobe, but the arthritis had vanished like a lost soul, and Satan was on his lawyer before Benny could react. "I don't know, sir! Search is up and we're coming online!" Benny assured him as Satan brushed him aside and charged on through the control room.

Benny fell in on his heels and rounded the first row of consoles.

"I've got it!" someone yelled from across the room.

Satan rounded another corner. "Playback! I want playback!" he barked.

"I've got it, sir, I've got it! It's a kid!"

It was Bleeder's sector, and he was on it remarkably fast to be on a level-three auto-scan, Benny thought.

They stopped at Bleeder's cubicle. "Everything's okay, sir. It's just a little girl. She was praying for you," the gaunt man offered with a cunning smile.

"She was *what*?" the Devil said in disbelief. He squinted through his bifocals and peered over Bleeder's shoulder at the monitor.

"Praying for you, sir. She was praying for you," Bleeder said.

Satan broke his concentration on the screen and looked at Benny, whose attention was riveted to Bleeder's monitor. "Well, isn't that nice," he said sarcastically, leaning forward again to glare at the little girl asleep in her bed. "Good work, Bleeder," the Devil said to himself in a calm voice. "Why would a little girl be prayin' for the Devil...?"

He straightened up, pulled a cigar from the pocket of the old housecoat, stuck it into his mouth, and pointed it at Benny. "She woke me out of a dead sleep," he complained. "Make sure she doesn't do it again."

Benny broke out of his trance. "I'll take care of it, sir; right away," he said with authority.

"Hey, this is my sector. I can—"

"I said, I'll take care of it," Benny repeated, glaring down at the worthless child molester.

"Okay, okay," Bleeder said and snatched his hands away from the keyboard.

The Devil picked up on the tension between his lawyer and Bleeder. "You're workin' too hard, Benny," he finally said with a calculated tone. "You need to learn to delegate authority. Bleeder here's a good man."

"Yes, sir. Thank you, sir. I'll work on that. It's just that I feel responsible for things like this and like to take care of them personally," he said to remove any further doubt that he would handle the situation.

Benny waited for the sound of the stone door closing to tell him Satan was in his lair. "You got on that pretty fast, Bleeder. I don't think I've ever seen anybody get online that quick," Benny said in a complimentary voice. "What about that, guys, any of you ever get up and running that quick?"

The other members of the crew shook their heads.

The one they called Bleeder gave Benny a sullen look. "Maybe that's 'cause I'm sharp," he said.

Benny scanned the other faces and dropped to one knee. He focused on the screen as he spoke and did not make eye contact with the convicted child murderer. "No, I'll tell you what it is, Bleeder," he said, with a confidential tone. "I think you were already online, and I think you were stalking the little girl on your own time, and I think when you're not running a sanctioned operation you need to stay off the board or I'll have you roasting on a spit." He stood and surveyed the faces around him. "That's what I think, and it'll pay you and everyone in this place to think the same thing."

4

Monday, December 2

"An angel of the Lord appeared to them," Katie said.

She stood above and behind The Three Shepherds on the small stage on a riser made to look like a stone, her arm extended out over them. A background of a starry night sky hung behind them. "Do not be afraid. I bring you good news. Today a Savior has been born, and you will find Him in a manger in Bethlehem, wrapped in swaddling clothes."

With a play book in his hand, one of the peasant boys stood next to the makeshift field where the shepherds gathered around a small campfire. "So it was that the shepherds hurried to Bethlehem and found the baby Jesus in a stable," he read.

The shepherds moved from the field down to the stable to stand around Mary and Joseph seated at the manger. Katie stood behind and above them. "They worshipped Him saying," the boy continued, and then the shepherds said, "This is the Christ, about whom we have been told. Praise be unto His holy name, our Savior and Lord."

"Glory be to God in the highest," they all said in cadenced unison. "Peace on earth and good will toward men. Unto the world, a Savior is born that we may forever live in His light and be blessed by His love. Amen."

"And now everyone remains still for just a moment," Mrs. Barnett said, her hands held in a position of restraint, "while the lights go out...that's good...now don't anyone move," she said with a degree of urgency, "until the lights come back on...that's good, now...everyone take a bow," she said quickly.

"Wonderful! Wonderful!" She clapped her hands. "Everyone did such a good job! I'm so proud of all of you!

"Now, let's hurry," she said. "We're running a little late. Everyone gather around for our closing prayer." The kids scurried about trying to get into place. "That's good, that's good. Now, next time we'll go through the whole play without our play books and see if we all remember our lines. Until then, practice, practice, practice! Okay, let's pray." She placed her hands together and bowed her head, looking over the top of her glasses to make sure every head was bowed and every eye closed. When she began the prayer, Katie and the rest of the kids joined in.

"Dear God, thank you for your precious love, and all our blessings from above. Thank you for the food we eat, the friends we keep, and for watching over us while we sleep. God bless us all in the name of Jesus—"

"And God bless the Devil—"

"Amen."

Every head in the room popped up.

Satan stood behind the Kid's console with Benny and a small crowd of onlookers, his arms folded across his chest, following the conversation between the two girls on the screen.

"I can't believe you did that."

It was Carol Adams, Katie's closest friend. They were standing in front of the church on the cleared sidewalk waiting for Katie's mother to pick them up. The boys in their group were preoccupied with a snowball battle under the amber glow of sodium vapor streetlights in the churchyard. The last rays of a dense, rust-colored sun transformed the clouds in the western sky into lavender and red streaks. Carol glanced around before she spoke. "You better cut that stuff out before your mom takes you to see that crazy preacher."

"Mr. Frey is a nice person," Katie said.

Her friend made a face. "You'll think he's nice when he puts some kind of spell on you."

Satan backhanded Benny in the chest. "The kid's smart," he said casually. "That preacher really is a bozo." He frowned with distaste. "What is it that makes them that way?"

Several heads shook in unison.

"I think the Devil would be a nice person if everyone would pray for him and be nice to him," Katie said.

"I don't think anyone that mean wants to be prayed for," her friend said, methodically pressing her footprints into the snow.

"But if everyone prayed for him and wanted to be his friend, maybe he wouldn't need to be so mean," Katie said. "No one likes him. I know I wouldn't be very happy if no one liked me."

"Friends!" the Devil bellowed with laughter. With obvious disgust, he surveyed the small group huddled around him. "Now, what do I need with friends when I've got you guys around?"

His cronies straightened up and beamed

smiles at one another in response to the imagined compliment.

"I never thought about it that way," Carol said.

"He probably doesn't have a Christmas tree, or get Christmas presents or cards, or anything. And the Bible says he's very old," Katie said. "All his friends have probably died by now. He must be terribly lonely."

The Devil raised his eyebrows. A snicker surfaced somewhere in the group. All his cronies glanced at him as inconspicuously as possible and tried to ignore the obvious pain the girl's remark caused him. A wicked grin formed on the Devil's face. "That's all right," he said maliciously, "she'll get old someday, too."

"If everyone prayed for him and he had lots of friends, maybe he would feel better and be a happier person. That's why I'm going to pray for him, because he needs help, and I'm going to be his friend."

The sneer on Satan's face dissolved into blank surprise. "She's serious," he said with a deadpan reaction. "With Christmas comin', you'd think a kid that age would have somethin' to think about besides prayin' for the Devil."

General nods of agreement.

"Apparently she doesn't," the Devil said, almost to himself. He snapped his fingers at the Kid's screen and it went blank. "I wanna see you in my office, Benny. The rest of you get back to work," he grumbled, "this ain't the Fourth of July."

Benny stood in his usual spot in front of the coffee table in the Devil's chamber, unable to relax, with the feeling of a massive foot crushing his chest.

"I don't like this," the Devil said. He paced like a wild animal in a cage, waving the cigar in the stifling air as he spoke.

"She's just a little girl, sir. I'm sure she doesn't mean any harm."

The Devil continued his pacing, deep in thought. "You don't get where I am by takin' things for granted. I don't trust anybody—not even you—because I can't afford to. I'm the Devil. My job is to question everything."

He poked the cigar at Benny. "You see, it's not the girl I'm afraid of; it's God." He stopped abruptly and held up a finger. "Let me take that back. I ain't afraid of anybody. But God has a lot of power, and He works in," the Devil did a little flourish with his hand, "mysterious ways. You have to watch Him or He'll get ahead of you in this game of universal exploitation. I can handle the zealots and all those idiots on television, 'cause they have something I can use against them: Fear. The girl is innocent. She ain't got a clue as to who I really am, therefore she has no reason to fear me. Put God behind her, and that lack of fear makes her dangerous."

The Devil wandered over to the Overlook and peered into the flames. "We have to give her a reason to fear me." The reddish flicker behind Satan caused his silhouette to pulsate. "Put somebody on it right away. Give her a number and put her on the board. Run a trace on her for a week and keep an eye on her."

"Yes, sir. I'll handle it personally, sir."

"No," the Devil said quickly. "You can put somebody else on it; I want you workin' on other things."

"Sir, if it's that important to you, I'd like to handle it myself to make sure nothing goes wrong," Benny said with a little more force than he expected.

Satan picked up on the assertive response. He met Benny's eyes for a terrible brief moment, and finally said, "Okay...just get on it."

Benny fell against the black door after it sealed Satan inside his lair. "What am I gonna do now?" he whispered. She had Satan's attention. Not good, he thought. Satan wouldn't leave a thing alone once it got his attention, and this was one thing Satan would have to leave alone. "Damn,

Katie," he said, pushing himself off the hot door, "Why can't you just be a normal, scared little kid?"

...bless the Devil.... God bless the Devil....

Satan wrenched himself out of the dream and sat up in his bed with an anguishing cry. "What...? What! Who's there! Who's..."

The red light on the wall in his bedroom pulsed with quiet urgency, fading into and out of the cobwebs in his head. "There?" he finished. "Who's there?" He sat in the darkness with his head between his knees, the two prayers rumbling through his head. "Go away and leave me alone."

Tuesday, December 3

"A good attorney does his research. You understand the importance of quality research don't you, Counselor?"

"Yes, sir." Benny stood at attention, appearing tired.

Satan reclined comfortably in his old chair.

The room stank with uncertainty.

"Well," Satan said, "I'm no hotshot attorney like you," looking up with a smile, "but I do my research." He pitched a folder onto the coffee table and stood.

In big red letters on the cover of the black folder, Benny's name glowed like a fresh brand.

Satan paced; Benny didn't move. "Now, I'm not much of a family man," Satan said, "so I need you to help me work through this." Hours seemed to pass before he spoke again. "My records," he pointed to the folder, "tell me your last name used to be Hart. Is that correct?"

Benny swallowed hard. "Yes, sir. That's correct."

"Uh huh," Satan replied absently. "And my records also show that you have a brother named Paul."

"Yes, sir."

"And brother Paul has a daughter named Katie." Satan paced, feigning concentration on his logic.

"Yes, sir."

"And brother Paul's little Katie is the same little Katie who is prayin' for the Devil...."

"Yes, sir," Benny admitted.

Satan laughed.

"So that makes you," the left forefinger shot toward Benny, its long, pointed nail a death arrow aimed at his soul, "her dear uncle.... Did I get it right, Counselor?"

Sweat poured off Benny's face, his head a

sponge Satan had just squeezed. "Uh, yes, sir. I'd say you got it right, sir," he said with a defeated sigh.

"Well then," Satan proclaimed, "I did good, didn't I?"

Silence.

"Seems to me we might have what you'd call a conflict of interest here," Satan followed up. "You think that's a problem?"

There was only one answer. "No, sir."

Silence again.

"Why wasn't I told about this?"

"Sir, I didn't think you needed to be concerned with—"

"I need to be concerned with *everything*, Counselor. Every single, minute detail of existence is my concern."

"Yes, sir, but I assure you it has no bearing on how I'm handling the situation."

"Oh?" Satan appeared surprised. "Is that so?" The Devil pointed the cigar at Benny, his face still calm and relaxed. "You don't appear to be handling the situation at all. A few days ago, we had one little innocent savior, now we got two of 'em, and one of 'em praying for me in the church. That's not good."

Satan sauntered up so close to his face that Benny couldn't focus on him. "You want the operation? Then I'm gonna give it to you—officially," he said with a challenging tone. "Let's see how strong you are," the Devil said. "I've given you enormous power. Let's see if you can use it. Let's see if you can do what you do best. You know, be the professional you are and remove your emotions from the case. I wanna see you," Satan grabbed Benny by the throat and buried the pointed fingernail into the side of his neck, "go for the jugular, Counselor!"

His eyes bored into Benny's mind. "You get your little brat niece off my back, or I'll do it for you," the Devil hissed into his ear.

Satan released his grip and moved to the coffee table while Benny coughed and hacked. He flipped open the humidor. "Cigar?" he said casually, offering one to Benny.

Benny rubbed his neck and tried to gain control of his breathing. "No, thank you...sir," he managed. "Sir, Katie's not a threat, she's just—"

"Dangerous!" the Devil shouted, slamming the humidor lid shut and turning on him. "Dangerous, dangerous, *dangerous*! And I don't need you to tell me who's a threat and who's not!"

"Yes—"

"Do you understand me!"

"—Sir."

Satan's words echoed off the walls, died, leaving a terrifying silence in their place. He approached the Overlook and watched the flames for what seemed an eternity before he spoke. "I cannot allow this to get out of hand, Benny," the Devil said softly, his silhouette flickering in the darkness. "The ramifications are staggering. You better deal with it."

Wednesday, December 4

Benny sat in the darkness with his face in his hands and his elbows on the console and watched Katie roll around in the snow with the dog. So happy, so unspoiled by the realities of the dangerous world that lurked just outside the protective walls of her innocence. Perhaps if she understood those realities she'd back off. But what could he tell her? The Old Man had left him with only one indication of the magnitude and scope of the situation: "The ramifications are staggering."

That was enough. Operating at Satan's level, such a statement had universal dimensions, but how would he get that across to Katie?

He had to find a way. This praying-for-the-Devil business could not continue. "Katie darling, don't you understand? You can't be doing this," he pleaded to the screen. Of course she didn't understand; she was only eight years old!

If she made the Old Man mad, he'd go after her. If she did this again, he'd have to use all the powers allocated to him by Satan to reach her. He'd have to...*give her a reason to fear me....* Although he didn't have any idea as to how to go about doing that, the alternative could be disastrous.

He focused on the screen, forcing his thoughts through the glass, through the dimensional walls and the warp that separated his world from hers, until...until that stupid little dog growled at the screen.

Benny bared his teeth and returned the growl.

"Hey, Benny."

Benny tensed and whirled around in his chair.

The Kid stood behind him.

"Hey. What's up," Benny said, straightening up, trying to divert the Kid's attention from the screen.

The Kid checked his perimeter and said, "What's the deal with the girl? I just got an op and a trace order on her."

"I know. I sent it." Benny told him about the meeting with Satan. "I want this op isolated."

"No problem," the Kid said. "What's the big deal?"

Benny drummed his fingers on his console. "I'm her uncle," he said. He thought the revelation might build a fire under the Kid. He was right.

The Kid's eyes grew large. "So that's what it is! Cool!" he said, grabbing Benny by the arm and shaking him.

Benny relaxed a bit at the thought of having someone he could trust, someone with whom to share the burden. "Yeah," he said. "I fell in love with her the day they brought her home from the hospital."

Benny sighed. "She's the daughter I never had." He spun around in his chair. Katie played across the screen. "I used to buy her books." He smiled as the memory took him back to better times. "I remember one Christmas when I spent the night with them and helped her father set up her new swing set on Christmas Eve." He chuckled. "We worked on that thing all night.

"I was crashed out on the couch early the next morning when she ran in and flopped down under the Christmas tree. She searched through all the presents, even the ones Santa had brought her, until she found the one from me. She opened it up, and with a smile that would melt steel, said one word: 'Books!'

"I'll never forget that day, Kid. It's the only time I ever cried." He pointed to the screen. "And that little girl is the only woman I've ever loved."

Benny ran his hands through his hair. "What am I gonna do?" he said, watching Katie chase the dog across the screen. "I've got to find a way to get the Old Man off her mind."

The Kid pondered Benny's dilemma while he studied the screen. "Maybe we could put that preacher onto her. Surely he could say something stupid enough to scare her. Maybe they could build her a playhouse or something. Or what if her mother got pregnant! A baby brother or sister would give her something else to think about."

Benny smiled. "Thanks, Kid."

The dog barked and leaped at the screen.

"I think you got his attention," the Kid said.

Benny gazed into the Kid's eyes.

"The dog," the Kid said, pointing to the screen, "I was talking about the dog."

"Oh, yeah," Benny said quickly, remembering his history with the dog. "That little runt used to bite me every time I'd go over to see her."

The Kid scratched his head. "Maybe somebody else ought to be running this one, Benny."

Had the remark come from another crew member, Benny would have considered it a threat, but the Kid was right. He was too close to Katie to handle this effectively. He also was too close to Katie to let anyone *else* deal with it. "I'll handle it," Benny said. "Somehow, I'll find a way to handle it."

"Kids her age don't have very long attention spans," the Kid said. "Maybe she'll lose interest."

"Yeah," Benny sighed, knowing she was too much like her uncle for that to happen any time soon. He rubbed his face. "I don't know, Kid. I just don't know.... Maybe she will."

☙ 5 ☙

Thursday, December 5

The dog was in the house. Benny had made sure of that.

Katie was alone in the backyard working on her snowman on this gloomy afternoon. She stood on a small stool, placing a baseball cap on his head. After meticulously positioning the hat where she wanted it, she began pinning it down with long spikes her father had made from wire clothes hangers.

Dense, smutty clouds pressed against the earth and against Benny's thoughts on this day, reinforcing his dismal mood and dulling his resolve to make the connection with her. His intrusion into her life had to be minimal, yet effective. At her age, he had to grab her attention and leave her with an indelible image she would remember and associate with his message, which was why he had chosen her backyard and the snowman for the encounter. While Satan's words hovered over his apprehensions, his hand hovered over the transport button on his console that would take him to Katie. Realization of the potential consequences she faced if he didn't do something forced him to push the button and step through the space-time differential between their worlds.

"Hi, Katie."

Satisfied with her work, she stepped down off the stool. Had the snowman spoken to her? She stepped back. Had he made the familiar sounds...? Snowmen couldn't talk, especially this one, because he didn't have a mouth yet. She glanced around, then returned her attention to the snowman. He seemed to be smiling, even without a mouth, and his immense black eyes sparkled with happiness. "Hello," she said. "Who are you?"

Benny spoke in a gruff voice. "I'm the Devil's friend, and I've come to tell you something he wants you to know."

"I didn't think he had any friends," she said.

"Well, that's one of the things I came to tell you. He's got *lots* of friends, he's very happy, and he wants you to know that you don't need to pray for him anymore."

"I don't understand that," she said. "The Bible says he's a mean person, that no one likes him, and that he's causing all the trouble in the world. If that's true, we should pray for him."

Did he dare tell her that stuff wasn't true? Did he dare plant such a dangerous seed in her fertile mind? You should either pray for the Devil or you shouldn't pray for the Devil....

The dog's sudden frantic barking from inside the house competed for his attention and compressed his time window. "Well, he's the Devil," Benny assured her. "He's *supposed* to be mean, so you don't need to pray for him anymore."

"I don't understand that, either," she said. "Why does he have to be mean? No one else has to be mean."

Exactly. He should have known better the instant he said it. *She'd make a fine lawyer....*

Just as Benny was about to try and explain that away, he was saved by, "Are you from Hell?"

Katie's mother appeared at the kitchen door, peering through the glass into the backyard.

"Yes," Benny said. "I am."

"Oh, good! Then, maybe you know my Uncle Benny," Katie said delightedly. "I think that's where he lives now."

Benny chuckled. "And what makes you think that?"

"Because Daddy said that's where Uncle Benny went to live when that mean man he was trying to help shot him," she said with perfect ease.

Benny's eyebrows leaped up.

"When I grow up, I want to be an attorney," she said, "just like my Uncle Benny, so I can help people like he did. If you see him when you get back home, would you please tell him that I love him and that I miss him a lot?"

That was the end of Benny's resolve. The situation fell apart before his eyes.

The kitchen storm door swung open. The mother was asking Katie who she was talking to. The dog was charging at them.

"Yes, sweetheart, if I see him I'll tell him that," he said.

Benny faded from her consciousness just as the dog leaped past her and into the air with its jaws snapping.

Six hours and seventeen minutes later, at precisely 8:37 p.m. Eastern Standard Time in the real world, with Benny's attention riveted to his computer screen, Katie Hart lay in her bed with the dog and her bear, and her mother at her side, and prayed for Satan's deliverance.

Benny slammed his fists down on the console and watched her image dissolve into the black void as the emergency alarm pierced his ears.

Friday, December 6

Satan stood behind the couch, his back to Benny, his attention fixed on the face of a child that floated in the flames beyond the Overlook. Or was it the face of God disguised as a child...? "She doesn't listen very well, does she?"

Benny wiped the sweat away from his face. "Uh, no, sir. She's pretty much an independent thinker, sir."

Satan huffed at the glass. "Just what we need," he said, "an eight-year-old independent thinker."

Silence.

"Well, I don't believe she's listenin' because I don't think she's the one doin' the thinkin'. There's somethin' goin' on here," he said in a menacing tone. "You tell me," he demanded. "You tell me that God's not up to somethin'. We got an eight-year-old brat who should have the attention span of a protozoan, and she's still on my back. Not only that, she's got her own little," his hand fanned the air, "Save-The-Devil campaign goin'. Now, you wanna tell me God's not behind this?"

So simple, Benny thought. God was either using Katie, or Katie was working on her own. If Satan thought it was God, maybe he'd just go after Him and leave Katie alone. If he thought it was Katie, maybe he'd just write it off as a child's fantasy and forget about it. Satan had no reason to fear a child; he had every reason to fear God.

If God wasn't involved, what power could a child possibly have over Satan? Maybe God *was* up to something. If that was the case, there was only one problem: He was working through Katie. Either way, Katie had Satan's attention, and that was a bad thing to have.

"Yeah, that's right," Satan said after a short silence. "Run a surveillance tap on all transmissions from Heaven that are directed to the girl, and transfer any suspicious encryption to my console." The Devil chuckled. "You see, He thinks I'm gettin' old, dryin' out. Thought He'd come after me disguised as an innocent little child—and He calls *me* evil."

Satan paced quietly, nodding affirmation of his insightful assessment. "Now," he said, "we have another problem." He glanced over his shoulder at Benny. "You went to see her?"

"Yes, sir."

"And did you tell her about her Uncle Benny? Did you tell her you successfully defended some of Organized Crime's most vicious leaders?"

Benny forced the incriminating words out of his mouth. "No, sir. I didn't tell her that."

"You didn't tell her you used to throw lavish parties for your friends, the urban wild dogs of the night, and finance them with payoffs?"

"No, sir."

"That you somehow convinced a jury that two of your clients—known hit men, who killed a young boy and his mother in the crossfire of a mob killing—were innocent?"

Benny didn't answer, couldn't answer.

"Don't you think you might have made a difference if you'd told her all that?" Satan stopped to make the point. "If she knew her Uncle Benny was evil, like me, she might turn sour and forget about the Devil. But then," he weighed the statement, "if she knew about her Uncle Benny she'd be heart-broken, and that might destroy her faith in the system. She might give up and go off the deep end, like her uncle did....

"You see where I'm comin' from, Benny? You're weak. You don't have what it takes to do this job. That's why I'm takin' you off the case. You're good, and that's one reason you stand at my right hand. But this one's over your head. God's powerful, and I don't trust Him with you. Don't worry, you're not gonna lose your job," Satan scoffed. "I just don't think you can handle God.

After all," he added with disgust, "you were only human."

"Sir, I think the Kid would do an excellent job—"

"Nah, this is between me and God," Satan cut in, "and I can't afford to take anything for granted when I'm dealin' with Him. There's too much at stake."

"But, sir, they're just a couple of little kids praying for you."

"Well I don't need anybody prayin' for me! Don't you get it?" Satan stormed. "A week ago we had one doin' it, now we got two doin' it. Where's it gonna stop? How long do we have to let it go before it gets totally out of control? This is a direct attack on who I am. I'm the Devil!" he cried, popping his chest with a finger. "I don't *need* anybody's sympathy!"

The room fell silent but for the ever present cracking of stone under Hell's torturous heat.

When Satan spoke again, the voice was calm, methodical. "In the beginning I thought it might just be the girl. You know, a kid's game. But we're in the big leagues now," he said to some distant ear. "We're not just dealin' with this little kid; we're dealin' with God, so we're gonna change the rules of the game. I'm takin' over. Now get outta here."

6

Saturday, December 7

Satan's bathroom was a cramped affair, stone, dark, painfully utilitarian, its requisite fixtures nothing more than minimal stone extensions of the walls that defined it.

Satan lingered there now, peering into the virtual mirror over his tiny sink basin. Using strategically placed fingers, he stretched the ancient skin and watched the scars of time that carved his face disappear, only to watch them surface once again when he let go. "This wasn't supposed to happen," he said to the apparition before him. He continued to stretch and admire the fleeting results.

"I thought I was supposed to stay young and handsome forever." He let go for the last time and issued a great sigh. "That's where it pays to read the contract."

He straightened up. So much for that bit of wisdom. The contract also didn't say he wouldn't suffer the wrath of arthritis, or that his hair wouldn't turn gray and fall out. He stroked what was left of his once beautiful hair and watched the ancient silver strands fall from his fingers. Where had the eons gone...? Up in smoke. He snarled at the ghastly image in the glass and willed the light to death.

He wandered into his chamber and stopped in front of the main screen that dominated The Wall, his attention intensely focused on Katie Hart. She ran through the snow with an old piece of knotted cloth in her hand and the mutt on her heels. She flailed the cloth about wildly, while the dog chased it with abandon, her giggling, the dog barking and snapping. A shame dogs don't go to Hell, he thought. He'd always wanted a nice dog....

But what did he really want? He had everything in the known universe—except the things that really mattered. Simple things like...horns, one true friend, somebody he could trust, somebody he could share his only secret with, peace...things that had slipped away through the coarse sieve of politics and power.

And what she had. The thing he missed the most, that endless and delightful innocence of youth, that magical time when responsibility was nothing more than a word in the dictionary. A time when life was fresh and raw and he walked along the banks of the Crystal River of Life, hand-in-hand with God, listening with childhood wonder to the story of creation....

Shut up!

Power and politics, those had been his passion and his game. Those two things had become his cold, lonely companions in life, bringing him to stand here alone in front of his virtual window onto existence, contemplating the course of action he would take against an eight-year-old child....

What a life.

There was a time when he conquered universes, brought civilizations to their knees, destroyed religions, even entire races of humans, and poured the fires of Hell across the land. His victories were fleeting now, shallow, insignificant remnants of the intoxicating glory days. It had all been done. He spent his time nowadays exercising variations on a theme, every day, reinventing the wheel in an endless downward spiral. He had reduced himself to a battle with a child, to a custodian directing traffic in the tamed corridors of a universe gone to Hell.

Oh, well, it was his job.

Yeah, that's what it was, a job, a position in time that offered no way out and nowhere to go but down.

As he watched the screen, dusk was about to claim her world. The outline of her house, the evergreens in the yard, winked on. Christmas lights on a timer. A brilliant, hellish sun hung low behind the barren trees to the west, its rays thousands of jagged red blades slicing up the frozen landscape. The earth looked as though it would rupture and bleed to death at any moment.

And there she was, his fragile, beautiful little nemesis, whirling through the dying swords, oblivious to the impact of her intentions and the consequences she would suffer because of them.

He yawned and snapped his fingers at the screen.

Nothing happened.

He stood there for a moment, looking at his fingers, at the screen, back at the fingers.

He snapped them again; the screen winked out.

Satan shrugged wearily and wandered off to bed.

Lucifer and his friends emerged like a flurry of butterflies from a delightful flower garden that bordered the River of Life opposite the great Light of God. Giggling and leaping about, flowers falling from their hair, they all skipped to the shoreline, and protected by their innocence, danced across the great luminescent ribbon, whirling about in the Light.

It wasn't actually a river, but an endless, winding presence, pulsating with God's love. Rainbows of color streamed from its surface into the sky in great fountains of light and curled outward into a misty, opalescent, universal shower.

Armed with truth beyond his years, Lucifer stopped at the shoreline, longing to join his friends—friends who were slipping away from him—yet unable to follow them. On his walks with God, it was from this very source, this river of knowledge, that he learned the things that now prevented him from chasing his friends across it. That knowledge would rob him of his youth and soon place him at the left hand of his God.

They teased him for being a silly boy. "Oh, do join us Lucifer," Mariah called. "We're having such fun!" She stretched out her hands toward him.

She was radiant beyond the imagination, silken hair streaming about her, loving eyes a heavenly blue that mesmerized him. He smiled, unable to explain his reluctance to join her, unable to pour his soul out to the tender heart he loved so dearly.

They were floating now, singing, gliding through the colorful ribbons of light. How he longed to join them, to laugh and dance with them, to hold her hand in his and openly profess his love for her to the heavens.

But he couldn't. He had to wean himself of her presence, of her thoughts, her love, of everything that she was or ever would be to him. His time would soon come to know the Truth, to know what God knew, and when that happened, the enchanting sweetness of youth—and his Mariah—would slip beyond his grasp forever.

With that sad thought to urge him on, and to the delight of his companions, he stepped onto the flickering surface and ran leaping with abandon toward them.

They all ran to meet him, grabbing each other's hands and whirling in a circle, singing and dancing. Euphoric, he danced, Mariah's hand in his, infused with her love—

"*...you for being my friend, God bless Mommy and Daddy and Freebie, and God bless the Devil, Amen.*"

—until one of her hands slipped from his grasp, and the circle cracked, and they were drifting away from him, reaching, calling, dissolving into ghostly apparitions.

"Come back! Please come back, Mariah!"

he cried, her face now distorted by fear. His last remembrance of her was her brilliant blue eyes glowing like stars in a frozen night, an image that would sear his memory for all eternity.

When the screaming stopped and the heavens and the universe fell quiet, he stood alone on a vast pulsating plain. It began to boil and roll and groan and rise around him, stretching forever away from him on all sides.

The glittering surface churned underneath his feet as he fought to keep his balance.

He broke into a run, struggling to reach the shore, leaping from one seemingly solid bit of ground to another, each one falling away the instant his foot struck it.

He sank, down, down.

Black smoke invaded his nostrils.

Great reddish vortexes twisted out of the inferno and shot up around him, darting, bleeding tongues licking away the heavens. With a fury that rivalled the fires of Hell, the sacred river suddenly burst into flames.

Katie's face appeared, trapped in the holocaust. He screamed "No!" and lunged for her and flung himself awake in his bed.

Sunday, December 8

A bright, frigid day greeted Satan. Strong winds had blown the clouds away the night before and left a crisp blue sky in their wake. Earth's shadows, black and razor-edged, appeared etched into the white, frozen world. How he longed to feel the cold just once....

Katie stood in front of the snowman with a handful of black plastic jar tops in her hands. He watched the girl's frosted breath rising around her face. It was the face in his dream. He had thought the dreams were gone for good. So long had it been since the images and the pain had virtually incapacitated him, driven him to madness after his exile. Of course, he had never forgotten the pain, or the madness, or Mariah, and he never would. He had simply buried the tender memories under vast, thick layers of time and volcanic evil in an attempt to kill them forever. Now they were back; he knew why, and it would have to stop.

"Hey, kid."

Katie stopped placing the jar-top buttons on her snowman.

"Yeah, that's right; I'm talkin' to you."

She hesitated for only a moment. "Snowmen can't talk," she said with certainty.

Stupid kid. Don't you have any sense of imagination? Anybody else her age would have been delighted that a snowman could talk, Satan thought. "Well, I ain't the snowman," he said in a menacing tone, "I'm the Devil."

Her little face brightened. "Oh, you're Mr. Devil?" she said with surprise. "Then I have lots of questions to ask you, but," she tipped her head sideways, "how do I know you're the Devil?"

"Mr. Devil." Satan muttered the words. "Because I said so," he shot back. "Now look, kid, you gotta stop this prayin' for me business, you understand?"

"If you're Mr. Devil, why don't you have horns?"

"There, you see," Satan mumbled to himself, looking around to see if anybody was listening. "I've said it forever: I need horns. I just don't," he said louder, "and I don't like it any more than you do. Now—"

"Do you know my Uncle Benny?"

Satan rolled his eyes. "Stupid kid ain't heard a word I've said. Yes," he said, "I know your Uncle Benny, now shut up and pay attention. You—"

"Is he mean?"

"What! What is this? Of course he's mean. Why do you think he went to Hell?"

"He was never mean to me," Katie said.

Satan thought that one over. "Well, you don't have to be mean to everybody to be mean," he said.

"Why are *you* mean to everyone?"

He lowered his head and shook it. “You just don’t get it, do you? It’s my job,” Satan said. “That’s what I do.”

“Why don’t you get a different job?”

“Because I don’t want a different job,” he lied. “I like bein’ mean, if that’s all right with you? Look, we all got a job to do. My job is to be mean; your job is to be a kid and not worry about the Devil. So knock off this prayin’ business, and tell that little brat friend of yours to do the same or you’ll both be sorry.”

She appeared sad. “I’m sorry you don’t have horns,” she said pitifully. “It must be awful to be Mr. Devil and not have horns.”

Yeah, Satan thought. Such a seemingly minor thing if you weren’t the Devil, not having horns, but it was something he had never gotten over....

“I don’t suppose you get Christmas presents, do you?” And before he could answer, she said “Would you be a happier person if you had horns?”

Satan cocked up an eyebrow, and after having a second to think it over said, “Yeah. I’d be happier if I had horns.”

“Good,” Katie said. “Tomorrow you shall have them.” She pressed the last button into place. “I have to go inside now. I’m getting cold.” With that, she ran toward the house.

“Hey, wait a minute,” Satan shouted. “You come back here, I’m not finished! You can’t just run off like that," he complained. He watched the door close behind her. "And you stop that prayin' for me, you understand? I ain't gonna put up with it much longer."

She was so much like the little angel who once walked the banks of the River of Life and questioned everything in his path. He had paid a terrible price for his rebellious ways. Satan wondered what price Katie Hart would pay for hers.

As he dissolved into his journey back to the control center, he noticed movement behind the frosted glass in the kitchen door. It was a small hand waving back at him.

7

Monday, December 9

After ringing the doorbell, the Reverend Fred Frey waited patiently on the Hart's front porch. It was a fine house, one of those southern-style two-stories with a wraparound porch and dormers on the upper level. A yellow house with green shutters and holiday trimmings draped along the porch rails.

His visit would surprise them—intentionally. Not that he was trying to spy on them. He certainly had no reason to suspect that anything was wrong. As far as he knew, it was a fine family. The Harts were quiet, regular churchgoers of whom he'd never heard anything but good. He just wanted to get a random snapshot of their daily life. His main concern was the child.

The whole thing was odd. After giving it some thought on the drive over, he realized that he had never run across anything like this in his thirty-five years in the ministry.

God works in mysterious ways.... Was this intended, for some reason, to bring him closer to the Harts? A sign that something was wrong in the Hart household? God often worked through children to reach adults. Perhaps the child was trying to tell someone something, seeking help.

Abuse...? Surely not.

Shadows, door knob turning.

The porch light winked to life as the door opened. Whatever it was, God had sent him to this house, and God would light his way. "Good evening, Mrs. Hart."

"Reverend! What a surprise," Rachael Hart said, stepping aside. "Come in. Let me take your coat."

"Thank you, Rachael, thank you."

"What brings you out on such a cold night?"

"Well, I wanted to get by to see you," he explained, shedding the coat. "Seems...something's come up you might want to know about. Is, uh, Paul at home?"

"Yes, he is. Please come in." She ushered

him into the living room. "Paul is in the den, let me go get him."

He watched her disappear, a cheerful woman, dressed in muted warm colors, relaxed, happy to see him....

The large family Bible on the coffee table caught his eye. It didn't appear dusty—nothing in the room did. The living room was toasty, the fireplace crackling and hissing with the sound of real wood. Large red and white Christmas stockings with black toes hung from the dark wood mantle above the fireplace, one manly, one feminine, the one with a big Santa Claus on it definitely belonged to Katie—it already overflowed with Christmas goodies. A large living room, open and comfortable, furnished in a cozy country style, displayed generations of family photos. Judging from its cracked sepia finish, one in particular must have been the great-grandparents of one side of the family or the other.

Photos of Katie Hart dominated the room, reflecting not only the flicker of the warm fire, but her progression through the years. All bubbled with joy; none indicated an abused child. Another one, on a bookshelf to his left, revealed a flamboyantly dressed man wearing dark sunglasses and a dazzling smile, proudly squeezing a child he held in his arms. The child was Katie Hart; the man, not her father, was probably a relative, uncle perhaps. Her mouth was flung open in a wild display of delight.

The tart fragrance of evergreen permeated his nostrils. A robust, live Christmas tree stood in the far corner opposite the fireplace. A host of translucent angels picked up the color from rows of twinkling multi-colored lights strung across the tree's branches. A fine house, a house of love....

Paul Hart entered the room wearing a pair of simple khahi slacks and a checkered brown flannel shirt, house slippers, wife following him in.

"Reverend," he said with the same enthusiasm Rachael had displayed. He firmly shook the Reverend's hand. "How are you? Please have a seat."

"Would you like a cup of hot chocolate," Rachael said, "I just put some on for Katie and—"

"No. Thank you, Rachael," Reverend Frey said. "I won't take up a lot of your time. I came by to ask you about Katie. Is everything all right with her? She seems to be happy and all?"

The parents looked at one another, a slight hint of concern on Rachael's face. "Why, yes," they said, stumbling over each other's words as they sat together on the couch.

"What's the problem?" Paul asked.

"Well," Reverend Frey sat uncomfortably in a chair across from Paul, "it seems that Katie included Satan in her prayer after the play rehearsal at church, and I thought you might want to know that. Unless, of course," the Reverend said quickly, "you already know about it, and you don't need me over here interfering with your lives. I just thought if there's a problem I could—"

"No, we didn't know about it," Paul said, glancing at his wife, then back to the Reverend. "How did that come about?"

"Well, we don't know," the Reverend said after a pause. "I was hoping you could shed some light on—"

"She's been praying for him for over a week now," Rachael said.

"What?" Paul appeared baffled.

"Yes," Rachael said. She reached for his hand. "I was going to tell you about it, but I was hoping she'd give it up and I wouldn't have to. You know how kids are."

"Where'd she get a crazy idea like that?" Paul asked.

Rachael cast an apologetic look at Reverend Frey and spoke to her husband. "From Reverend Frey's message last Sunday," she said, now making eye contact with the preacher and trying to explain. "When you suggested we should pray for world leaders and people in power, she chose the Devil."

"Lord, have mercy," the Reverend declared.

"I tried to tell her she should pick someone else, but...well, she thinks he's the one who needs it the most," Rachael said in defense of her daughter. "And it makes perfect sense if you're a child," she continued. "If the Devil makes all the bad things in the world happen," she said, counting on her fingers, "and he's as mean as everyone says he is, and if he doesn't have any friends, then..." she shrugged. "Doesn't it make sense that he needs God more than anyone, and we should pray for him and try to be his friend?"

"Be his *friend*?" Paul said.

"Yes, she wants to be his friend."

"Lord, have mercy," the Reverend cried again.

"It's okay, it's okay," Rachael said to her husband. "It's just something she's going through. She'll get tired of it. I know she will." She wiped at an eye. "I just couldn't tell her she was wrong. She was so sincere and compassionate, and she spent so much time looking up scriptures in the Bible. I didn't know what to tell her, so I thought, what does it matter if she prays for the Devil for a few days? She'll get tired of it."

"It matters because she has Satan's attention," Reverend Frey said softly. "Has she been acting out stories...anything that looks like make believe?"

Quiet settled over the room, the pulsating multi-colored light from the Christmas tree playing across their faces.

"When I went outside the other day to check her progress on the snowman she's building, she was talking to herself. She told me that someone from Hell had come to see her and told her she didn't have to pray for the Devil anymore."

"What?"

"Lord, have mercy!"

"When I opened the door to check on her, poor little Freebie ran outside in a frenzy and leaped past Katie like an attack dog," Rachael said. "He acted like he saw something Katie couldn't see."

"Lord, have mercy!"

"Oh, for Pete's sake, Rachael, you know how protective Freebie is around—"

"She says she spoke to the Devil himself, Paul."

"She *what*?" Paul jumped up.

"Lord, have mercy on this precious child," the Reverend cried.

"Hey, what about a little mercy for me," Satan said, scanning the faces of his cronies while they watched the screen. "She's the one who started the whole thing."

"She named the snowman Mr. Devil," Rachael said.

"I'm afraid Satan is trying to possess your daughter."

"Oh, jeez, now don't tell 'em that, Fred!" Satan whined. "I ain't tryin' to possess anybody. You'd think this was *The Exorcist*. I just want the little brat to stop prayin' for me."

"Come on you two," Paul said. "This whole thing is getting a little ridiculous. Look, Reverend, I'm certain this is all a child's fantasy that Rachael's reading too much into, and Katie's just playing out some kind of—"

"No," Rachael cut in.

"Oh, sweetheart, you're just over-reacting."

"No I'm not!" Rachael shot back. "I'll show you. Come with me." She led them through the kitchen to the back door and flipped on the floodlights.

Katie's snowman appeared in the back yard, a silent sentry guarding his wintry domain. "He had one of Paul's baseball caps on yesterday. Now he's got these. Bless her heart. She used icicles," Rachael whispered.

"Oh, my God," Reverend Frey gasped. "He's got horns!"

Benny and his buddies snickered.

"And what's so funny about that," Satan demanded.

"Oh, nothing, sir," Benny said, trying to regain his composure. "It's just that...you always wanted horns. Now you got 'em. Merry Christmas, sir."

Satan showed his teeth in a display of disgust amid the laughter then flung his housecoat around himself and disappeared from the control room.

When the preacher got into his car to leave the Hart place, he immediately locked his door, expelled a deep breath, and attempted to purge himself of the anxiety that squeezed his heart.

The *Devil*!

He should have known. Satan had actually made contact with a child in this very backyard. The Evil Beast stalked this household. His presence hung in the night air like choking smog. So close. And it was all Reverend Fred Frey's fault. The thought consumed him as he drove away from the house and headed home.

No, not home but to his church, where he would humble himself at God's altar and pray for forgiveness for misleading an innocent child, and for guidance in what to do next.

His salvation was the fact that this was God's will. Everything was God's will, and at times like this, he had to remain focused on that very fact. This could be a test, a beacon in the night, an opportunity for God to demonstrate his unrelenting mercy, an omen of some pending disaster or extraordinary event. It could be any number of things he didn't understand.

But he'd been here before. Countless times God had appeared to him in strange and mysterious ways with a message, an insight, or a job to do. God's intent wasn't always clear, was often concealed within the framework of an event that required interpretation, an event designed to test the resolve and the commitment of the recipient to God's will. Some of his greatest insights had been delivered in the form of seeming disasters, which later manifested themselves into miraculous events that glorified God.

Something big, something...glorious was about to happen. The rapturous thought almost stopped his heart. "This is what doing God's work is all about," he said to himself. "And God has called upon me to do His will!" The exhilaration from that was bliss in its purest form. There was some greater good to be served here, and it was up to him to find guidance in God's light, to do the will of his God. "Praise be to God," he said.

Perhaps Satan was riding the crest of the wave, since he was on a roll lately. He often compared the Demon to sunspots, flaring up on occasion and going on a tear when he found a weak spot in the flanks of life. Where was the weak spot? What had sparked such an intense and targeted incident? What had this child done that forced

Satan to crawl out of his evil hole, expose himself, and outright attack her like this? Regardless of his motives, it was times like this—when Satan became intoxicated with power—that he was the most dangerous, and Reverend Fred Frey needed a plan.

"Glory hallelujah. Glory be to God."

But he knew better than to go this one alone. He would take the usual precautions and add Katie Hart to his prayer list. He also would talk to his spiritual leaders in the church and see to it that she got on their prayer lists as well.

"And you need to arrange one of your little soirees at the Hart's house so you can try to talk some sense into God's head," Satan said. He rested his arms on the back of the front seat of Reverend Frey's car.

"I'll arrange for one of my special fellowship prayer meetings at the Hart's house," the Reverend told the windshield. These meetings were the centerpieces of his intervention program on behalf of families in need. He'd contact a select few of the Hart's church friends and arrange for each to bring a dish to the Hart's house on a given evening. They would all fellowship and eat and give witness to the glory of God in their own lives, tell stories of inspiration, share problems that each had overcome through the power of Jesus Christ, and then get down to some serious, unified and targeted prayer for the family in question. He had seen this technique work miracles in the past, and he needed a miracle now to save this helpless child from Satan.

"That's right, Fred. And maybe God'll give you a miracle and get this little brat off my back. But you gotta get on it quick."

"Christmas is right around the corner."

"That's right, Fred."

"I'll have to move fast. I need to get this resolved before Christmas Eve." Satan had no doubt chosen this busy time of year to act. People would be in a mad rush to finish off the ludicrous frenzy of Christmas shopping and traveling. Satan had timed his attack perfectly. Fred Frey would need something powerful. "Glory be to God. Get thee behind me, Satan!"

Satan patted the preacher on the shoulder. "I am behind you, Reverend, all the way. Now don't you worry about a thing. You just get your little fellowship goin', put a little pressure on God, He'll realize you screwed up, then He'll shut the girl up, and you and me are off the hook. Everything's gonna be all right."

Back in his lair behind the hot, black door and the evil that shielded him from the rest of the universe, Satan stood in the empty chamber and watched the girl on the operations screen, in her room, asleep.

Everything's gonna be all right....

He wasn't so sure.

The statement had lurked in the shadows of his mind ever since he'd made it. The child stalked the perimeter of his consciousness, a predator searching for a weakness in his defenses. The weakness was real, and the predator had found it. She just didn't recognize it....

The consequencies of such a recognition were unthinkable.

Satan paced methodically, chin in hand, alongside the Overlook, the dream vivid and animated in his head. As he walked, his old trunk floated in his peripheral vision.

Had God discovered the one weakness he had managed to conceal since his demise in The Beginning? Was that possible? Once more, he replayed the sequence of events that had expelled him from Heaven and brought him to stand here contemplating his fate. He could not find a single error in his logic. He had arrived in Hell with his fatal flaw safely tucked away behind a wall of hatred and had sheltered it with zealous vigilance.

Had God planted the idea of praying for the Devil in the girl's head through his trusty messenger, the Reverend Fred Frey? If so, that meant He knew. An eight-year-old child obsessed with praying for the Devil...? God almost had to be behind such a thing. Maybe He was just shooting into the dark, testing the fabric of time, probing for weak spots in the system. Not likely. God *was* the fabric of time. His existence was its very definition, the system itself. He either knew, or....

Maybe it was truly a fluke. A child's silly imagination, unpolluted by experience, took the good Reverend for his word and just picked the Devil out of the crowd. Possible? Yes. Likely? No. God might even be behind the prayers, but that didn't mean He understood their impact. The child certainly didn't. When he reached the wall, he stopped. Regardless of their source, the prayers would have to cease, and he had to shut the girl up without making a big deal of it.

His attention drifted toward the trunk that hunkered in its corner. *The dream.* Mariah had come back to him. He stepped down from the Overlook and knelt in front of the trunk, placed his hands on the rugged gold clasps that held it shut. The dreams of her had stopped shortly after his exile. Even then, they had persisted for eons. That had been his true Hell.

Her memory lay just beyond his fingertips, safe in the sacred pages of his diary. He closed his eyes. Her presence enveloped him, held his cheek against hers. And he knew what would happen if he lifted the lid on the trunk: the diary would be opened, the relevant pages would be read, and the torment of his loss would return. That could never happen.

The dream, the illusory voice of his angel, was not a harmless remembrance; it was an ominous warning from his past, a sign of weakness. Prayer, that insidious, malignant force, had gnawed a hole in his defenses during the night and allowed the predator to slip through under the cover of a dream. She was on the prowl inside the walls of his sanctuary, blind, innocent, unaware of her power. As much as he wanted to believe that everything would be all right, his gut, which had never failed him, leaped against its chain. Something was out there, something dangerous, an eight-year-old child. He removed his hands from the gold clasps and stood.

He faced the sleeping child on his monitor and snapped his fingers at the screen. Nothing happened. He did it again. Nothing.... He tried it several times. Nothing.

He rubbed his thumbs against his fingers. What was wrong? The system? Should he call the Kid?

No.

For the next few minutes he searched the lair for the remote control, in the old recliner, the bar, the bedroom, under the couch—where he finally found it.

He got to his feet, aimed the remote at the screen, pushed the POWER button. The girl disappeared.

Now he knew that everything would not be all right.

Wednesday, December 11

"Yes! Everyone is here now," Reverend Frey said cheerfully. The last couple on his list quickly stepped out of the night wind and across the threshold of the Hart's front door. "Praise Jesus. Come in, come in. How are you, Jim, Loren," he said, turning them toward the den.

Rachael relieved her friend of the casserole dish in her hands. "Thank you for coming," she said. "We appreciate everyone's support so much, and I know Katie would too if she understood."

"Well, that's okay," Loren said. "She doesn't have to understand right now. The important thing is that we understand. Is she here?"

"Oh, yes," Katie's mother assured the woman. "She's upstairs. We told her we were having some company over tonight, so she's going to get on the Internet for a while. Her little friend, Carol, is online too, and they just love the chat rooms on the WayCoolKids site. They can stay on it for hours."

"Well, good. We're so sorry this is happening," Loren said. "Maybe after tonight it'll all be over."

"Yes, I feel like tonight will be a turning point. Thank you," Rachael said. "Just make yourselves at home while I put this in the kitchen."

"You know the Goodmans," Reverend Frey was saying as he played the host and led them into the small group. "Yes, and our friends the Andersons over there, God bless them, made it in spite of the roads. What a fellowship this is."

Rachael made her way into the kitchen, where two of the men with plates in their hands discussed the new children's area at the church. She placed the food dish on the table and slipped down the hallway and upstairs to Katie's room.

"Okay!" she said, peeking through the door. "Everyone is here and you can have the line as long as you want it."

"Oh, good," Katie said. She saved her work in The Story Workshop and switched to the Internet sign on screen.

Her mother knelt and put her arms around her daughter and squeezed. "You know what," she said.

"What?" Katie replied, concentrating on the screen.

Her mother laughed and shook her. "A miracle is about to happen, because this is a special night, and we love you so much, that's what," she said, and kissed her on the cheek. "Where you going?"

"WayCoolKids," Katie said.

"Chat rooms?"

Katie nodded. "I think I'll try to find Sugarplum. I miss her a lot."

Her mother gave her another kiss. "Good, sweetheart. Have a good time. I'll be up in a little while."

As Katie Hart's mother left the room, love pushed a tear onto her cheek. She quietly pulled the door shut and leaned against it. She could not possibly know how incredibly accurate her earlier prediction would be.

Katie logged on to the Internet and typed *waycoolkids.com* and hit the ENTER key. She clicked on KID CONNECTION, then selected the CHAT ROOMS icon and typed in her password. When the little smiley-face came on the screen, she began typing.

Hello. This is Angel. Is anyone there...?

Downstairs, Reverend Fred Frey had everyone in an arm-in-arm kneeling circle for an opening prayer. "Praise be to God our Holy Father, the giver of all life. Lord, we come before you in this most troubling hour of darkness..."

Katie sat patiently and watched the empty INSTANT CHAT window on the screen while she pondered Reverend Frey's words. She had not been able to get what he'd said in church that day off her mind. The more she thought about it, the more it made sense. *Prayer is God's Internet, and love is God's World Wide Web.*

That's what he had said. And even though she didn't quite understand how it worked, God and Mr. Devil supposedly lived everywhere in the world. So if that was true, and the Internet was everywhere in the world, and prayer was God's Internet....

The screen flashed. Katie joyfully watched the words appear in front of her. *Hello Angel. It's nice to hear from you. This is your friend, Sugarplum. What have you been doing*?

"...so humbly request your intervention and mercy, oh gracious Lord, in the life of little Katie Hart..."

"Sugarplum!" Katie wiggled in her chair, excitedly trying to collect her thoughts, and then typed: *I'm very happy to hear from you Sugarplum. I've been playing with Freebie in the snow. That's a lot of fun. I've also been helping Mom bake sugar cookies. I'm getting good at it. I've been learning how to make snow ice cream. I'm still working on Snowman. And I have decided to be Mr. Devil's attorney.*

Then she smiled at the screen.

Please look at my Web site in a day or two. I have an idea that might change the world....

"...your precious and all-powerful hand on this innocent child and shield her from Satan!"

8

Friday, December 13

When Benny entered the sweltering room he found Satan standing in front of his operations screen, arms folded across his chest, watching the GNG evening news.

...extent of the damage, as yet, is not known, but company officials at WayCoolKids report that the entire Kids-In-Sync database, which controls all dynamic chat room activity on this network designed exclusively for kids, was wiped out. No one knows exactly what, or who, brought the system crashing...

Benny noticed that Satan used the remote

control to kill the screen; he also noticed that Satan picked up on his interest.

His arms crossed, Satan walked slowly to the Overlook. He stopped just short of the glass and peered into the fire. "She put it on the Internet," he said with a distinct lack of emotion.

He said it so quietly that Benny almost didn't hear him. "Yes, sir, the Internet, but I'm sure she didn't mean any harm, sir, she's just tryin' to do what she thinks—"

"She *put it on the Net*!" Satan roared, spinning around and lunging away from the glass. "We give her every chance! We warn her!" He advanced on Benny. "And while that stupid preacher and his sheep hold this," his arms flapped about, "big fellowship prayer meeting for her downstairs—"

"Yes, sir."

"She's *upstairs*," Satan swept the array of electronic gear on the long table under the operations screen into a spray on the floor, "exposin' her little plan to the whole world on a Web page on the damned *Internet*!" he exploded into Benny's face. "Do you know how many stupid little kids visit the WayCoolKids chat rooms?"

"Yes, sir. We got a count at thirty-two—"

"—million, eight hundred seventy six thousand, five hundred ninety three as of midnight last night!" Satan finished. "And where do you think these little angels-of-the-night are located?"

"Uh, all over the world, sir."

"That's right, and do you know how many of them accessed her Web page since night before last?"

Benny opened his mouth to speak.

"Two thousand eighty-three!" Satan boomed. "I had *two thousand eighty-three stupid little kids* prayin' for the Devil's salvation last night, and I don't wanna see that number get any bigger!"

"Sir, I don't understand why—"

"No you don't understand, do you? And when did you last have it explained to you?"

"Sir, I haven't—"

"That's right," Satan croaked, his nose now just two inches from Benny's ear. "And why is that? Maybe it's because it's not your job to understand."

"Yes, sir, that's exactly what it is!"

"Then why do you ask the question, Counselor?"

"Sir, I'm just tryin'—"

"To figure out what makes the Old Man tick?"

"No, sir! That's not it at all!" Benny cried, cowering from the creature developing before him.

Satan smiled through the distorted apparition, allowing silence to fill the void left by his tirade. "Then that's good," he said, his voice now deep and haunting. "We have reached another milestone in our relationship that I expect you to remember for a very long time."

"Yes, sir! Yes, sir!" Benny closed his eyes and sucked in a deep breath of the scorching air. "That's not a problem, sir, I'm deeply sorry...."

Satan backed off and crossed the room, his hands now clasped behind his back. "So the only record of what happened last night is in the minds of two thousand eighty-three other kids who know the Internet address of her Web site?"

Sweat poured off Benny's face. "Yes, sir. It would have taken too long to find each transmission in question, so we trashed the entire database. There's no record of any discussions in WayCoolKids chat rooms from four p.m. yesterday until now. I'm sure they have backups, but the failure will force them to verify the integrity of their backup procedures and test the system before they go back on line. Still, it's only a matter of time until they're back up to speed."

Satan cocked his head around. "So when they restore, we're back where we started?"

"Depends, sir. Maybe she'll back off now."

Satan shook his head. "She won't back off," he said to the Overlook.

Benny mopped the sweat off his face. "I'm sorry, sir. I thought if we disrupted the site it might give everyone something new to think about."

Satan waved off the comment. "Nah, that's

okay," he said. "I would've done the same thing. You did good." He leaned on the Overlook glass. "What have we got on God?"

"Nothing, sir. Complete silence."

"That doesn't make any sense at all," Satan said. "He must be gettin' to her somehow."

"Perhaps He's not, sir." Benny didn't know what Satan's problem was, but he knew his only chance of saving Katie was to convince Satan that God wasn't using her against him. And it was true. God wasn't using her, and Katie wasn't a threat, she was just a little girl trying to help the Devil.

Satan turned to Benny. "And what does that mean?"

"Well, maybe she's doing it on her own, sir."

Satan had considered that alternative before. "That's convenient. That would let our friend, God, off the hook."

"Yes, sir," Benny offered. "And it also would explain the absence of traffic. Unless He's come up with something you don't know about, He's not making contact with her."

Satan sneered at that. "So you think this little girl has a big heart, she's genuinely concerned about old Uncle Satan's welfare, and she's just tryin' to do him a favor?"

"Yes, sir. That's exactly what I think, sir," Benny said.

Satan paced and nodded, pursed his lips,

seemingly entertained by his own thoughts. "Well then, since she's the apparent *leader* of this little...movement," he said with a flourish of the hand, "we have to change her mind. If we can do that, the others will lose their will to fight and we can put an end to this nonsense. So, we have to stop her. You know...set an example." He stopped at the Overlook where the fires below played across his form like lightning. "I understand the little dog doesn't like you," he said.

"Yes, sir. That's correct."

"Good," Satan finally said. "Then we're gonna give your little Katie a reason to hate me. Who does she love more than anybody in the whole world?" he asked quietly.

Benny thought that one over, and with supreme confidence said, "Sir, I'd say that would be her mother."

Satan huffed at the flames below. "You idiot. That's why I'm the Devil and you're not.... Kill the dog," he said with a chilling absence of concern, "and blame it on me."

Benny couldn't contain his optimism. "Yes, *sir*!" he said. It was a harsh but absolutely brilliant solution. Killing Katie's beloved Freebie would hurt her terribly, but it also would turn her against Satan and spare her his wrath.

"I can't believe it. She gives me a nice pair of horns," Satan said, sadness molding his face, "then she puts me on the Net." He shook his head. "Get it done."

...God bless Mr. Devil...

...bless the Devil...

...to sleep, the Devil's soul I pray you keep.

Satan writhed under the covers, the images flashing one after the other in a fiery avalanche of paralyzing dreams that he could not outrun.

...make the Devil a good person.

"No, no," he moaned from the depths of his subconscious, winding himself up in the sheets, a powerless insect helplessly entangled in God's sticky web.

Dear God. Please help the Devil be good...

"Go away!"

...save the Devil...

...the Devil...

"No! Leave me alone!"

...from being a bad person.

Faces appeared in the flames, children's heads pouring out of the caldron, rolling down upon him. Great pillars of fire spewed from their eye sockets, blazing columns of death, whirling, pounding the earth, tumbling toward him. He ran—ever slower, it seemed—in a hopeless attempt to avoid being crushed by the fiendish heads.

...forgive the Devil.

His legs throbbed. He leaned into the run, arms out-stretched, his fingers tearing at the shiny darkness that hurtled away just beyond his reach, the darkness that would become his savior if he could somehow touch it, rip through it, plunge into the safety of the evil realm.

The heads closed in around him, towering wheels of fire pressing against him. He forced his body forward, reaching, his heels being sucked under the tumbling heads.

Smoke poured off his back. Flames! Pain beyond anything he had ever known.

Then suddenly, the demonic transformation began and the children reached for him and his finger touched the eternal wall, grabbing, clinging, his feet coming off the smoking earth. In one last, frantic attempt to save himself, he caught a breath, screamed, and lunged forward, plunging the pointed nail on his left forefinger into the void. With all the strength left in him, he hooked the finger into the fabric of time, yanked his body out of the pyre, and disappeared into the glorious abyss....

They were gone. Silence. Safety. Floating, drifting endlessly on the demonic wind.

He lay exhausted beneath the sheets, the blessed conversion now twisting his body, expelling the pain and the fear. He grunted in ecstasy. Slowly, the demon he had become rose up from the bed, the sheets sliding to the floor around it. With its head thrust toward Heaven, it issued a guttural, triumphant cry.

Its breathing coming in long pulls, it slowly turned to survey the room. The Beast moved toward the door and into the large chamber where the operations screen hung in darkness. It stopped at The Wall and straightened up, willing the gigantic screen to life.

On it, sound asleep in her bed, the image of little Katie Hart appeared. She lay on her side, a little pink bow still in her hair, the lace around the top of her pajamas ruffled up under her chin. Her hands rested beside her head, almost in a position of prayer, an innocent little angel intent upon saving her Devil.

The Demon contemplated the girl's image. A grotesque hand reached out to lightly touch the screen. With each breath, subtle wisps of flame drifted from its mouth and curled outward toward the child. It spoke in a slow growl. "Sleep, little one, and know this night that you must stop what you are doing. Your innocence leads you on a crusade that must fail, and from which there is no return." It gave a great sigh, and a gush of flames shot toward the screen. "You must leave me, little one. As you can see, I will not make a very good friend."

ॐ 9 ॐ

Saturday, December 14

Satan's voice blared over the intercom. "Benny, I'd like that progress report on the dog if you think you can find time to work it into your busy schedule."

"Yes, sir," Benny yelled, jerking his head toward Satan's lair. "It's on the way."

"No, wait," Benny said. He held the Kid's shoulder. "Let her get in the house so the dog won't be distracted...that's it," he said slowly, "keep going," motioning with his hand trying to help Katie up the back steps. "Boom! There goes the door."

Benny raised his head toward the intercom.

"Sir, if you'd like to watch your screen, we're going to bring that report to you live." He motioned to the Kid. "Do it."

Benny nudged Pusher. "Okay, Pusher, get in there and go."

Pusher typed, and his screen bloomed into an iridescent, bluish fog that radiated outward toward the wiry little man. Moments later, the eerie mist swirled around him and collapsed back into the screen, taking the Pusher with it.

Appearing along the wooden fence that bordered the large backyard of the Hart's house, Pusher checked his surroundings and spotted the dog lying on the porch.

"What if he only takes one bite of it?" the Kid questioned.

"Are you kidding," Benny gloated. "There's enough poison in that piece of meat to kill a bull elephant." He pointed to the screen. "Pay attention. Pull Pusher out of there as soon as he throws the meat. We don't want him to have any distractions."

"Oh, you won't have to worry about Pusher being dis—"

"The dog, you fool," Benny said to the Kid. "I'm talking about the *dog*."

Pusher took a last look around the quiet neighborhood and pulled a piece of meat from inside his old coat. Whistling, dangling the meat between his fingers, he threw it just over the fence. The dog raised his head, and Pusher vanished into the morning air.

"Here he comes, here he comes!" one of Benny's cronies said, squeezing the words past his teeth. They gathered around the Kid in wild anticipation, their eyes glued to the screen.

Being a dog, Freebie didn't have much of a grip on what was really going on from day to day. He just took things as they happened and didn't retain information that didn't have an immediate impact on his well-ordered existence. However, he knew what was in place and what was out of place in his neighborhood. As with all other animals programmed by evolution to survive in a world with no written rules, he was acutely aware of his personal space. His brain held a well-constructed blueprint of every sound, bush, odor, every nuance in the daily routine of every other animal—including humans—and every blade of grass between himself and the strange apparition that just threw something inside his invisible territorial boundary.

The event itself shocked his senses. First of all, none of the humans he knew ever stopped at the fence that marked that side of his territory and made that sound. Second, nothing that smelled like that had ever fallen into the yard. Strange goings-on indeed.

Whatever it was stood out like another dog in the snow. He approached the thing cautiously. The smell of blood bombarded his sensitive nose, not a scent he was accustomed to, since everything he ate came from inside the house.

The safe thing to do was walk around it, which he did when he got to it, to see if it moved, and certainly not to touch it until he had taken the precautions on his built-in survival checklist.

When he got close enough to it that his nose began to obstruct his view, the pungent smell pulled his eyes into slits. Satisfied that it was nothing in his best instinctive interest, he casually cocked his leg and did the only natural thing that marked it for avoidance.

The Devil snorted and nodded to the screen. "What a bunch of idiots. Good job, guys," he said louder to the intercom. "Excellent piece of work if I've ever seen it." He laid the remote control on the coffee table and plucked a fresh cigar from the humidor. "And, Benny," he called, wedging the cigar between his molars as he walked away, "you can forget that progress report on the dog."

"Uh, yes, sir."

Sunday, December 15

Katie carefully stuck a red candle into the cake in the center of the little devil figure she had drawn with the red icing. She thought the tail was a little long, but not by much. And as far as the candle was concerned, she had no idea how old he was—or if it was even his birthday. She just thought it looked nice.

"Finished," she said. She breathed deeply and glanced at the clock. A little over three hours. Not bad, considering she started from scratch and had to use her mom's kitchen step-stool to reach things. Satisfied with her work, she opened the kitchen door and returned for the cake.

Katie slowly made her way outside, both hands under the plate, and carefully down the steps to Snowman. She set the cake on the snow next to him, and after another trip into the house, a glass of milk and silverware.

She lit the candle. "There," she said, and looked up at the black eyes. "Are you in there?" She tipped her head, staring into the eyes. "I was hoping you'd come visit today. I baked it just for you." She licked a bit of icing off a finger. "I had a little trouble making the icing stick, but it's still okay," she assured him.

The remnants of cake mix and icing spotted her face, her forearms where she had reached around the cake to smooth the icing onto its sides, her hands, even her hair. Her apron was a mess from splashing around at the sink, and marked with brown smudges where she had carelessly wiped a finger or hand.

Satan gazed down at her. “I can’t believe it. It’s for me,” he said through a smile.

“I have to go now,” she said. “I hope you like the cake. And you can just leave everything where it is when you’re finished. I’ll come back and clean it up.”

His attention drifted back to the cake as she walked away, and all the things he would give just to taste it. But then, everything has a price, he thought. If he could taste the cake, he’d be able to taste other human attributes like weakness, mortality, pain, fear, and a host of other undesirable emotions...maybe even love for a little girl....

Movement caught his eye.

It was that stupid dog emerging from the shadow of a wicker chair and table on the back porch. He was looking directly at Snowman and the cake.

“Oh, no.”

The dog hopped down the steps.

“No,” Satan said, realizing the dog’s intentions. “Go away!”

Freebie trotted into the yard.

Satan began waving his arms about. “Go on,

get away from that cake, you stupid little mutt!"

Freebie didn't waiver.

Satan quickly transformed into a hideous demon and breathed a gush of fire onto the control room screen.

Freebie stopped. He scanned the yard looking for anything that didn't fit. Nothing. He glanced up at the snowman looming above him.

"That's right, it's me," Satan said.

Freebie growled.

Satan sneered at the dog. "You touch my cake and you'll be the first dog to burn in Hell."

Freebie eyed the cake. It was still warm. The sweet steam seeped into his nostrils. His eyes squeezed shut.

"No, no. Good dog. Come on now, don't do that!"

Freebie sneezed, instantly blowing out the candle. The temptation was simply more than he could stand. He stuck his nose to the cake and looked up at the snowman. A glob of brown frosting clung to the tip of his nose. His tongue whipped out and swiped it off.

Snowman's eyes flashed red. Satan glared down at the dog. "You'll pay for this one, buster."

"What have you got on transmissions from God to the girl?" Satan studied the screen on the

Kid's console, his arms folded across his chest in a display of absolute authority, while the remote control problem darted around in his thoughts like a terrified rat searching for a hole.

With Benny looking on, the Kid's fingers raked the keyboard. A split screen popped up. "Nothing, sir; no broadcast storms, no encrypted signals, no communication since we set up the routing audit."

Satan rubbed his chin. "Hmm. Maybe He's comin' to her from some other link?"

"No, sir," the Kid said. His fingers cut away at the keyboard again. "I've been tracking downloads and encrypted data bursts from all remote gateways and routable connections to her domain, sir. She's clean. The only way God's gonna get anything to her without us knowing about it is to take her to lunch."

"Yes," Satan said to himself. "I want that audit run for at least a week, to see if our trap produces a villain."

"Yes, sir," the Kid said. He glanced back at Benny. "Benny had me set that up a week ago, sir. We got the bases covered." He hit more keys. "We're running sector isolation with bandwidth priority alert on every relevant thread, i.e. the Reverend Fred Frey. If a data burst goes out we'll peg Him sir, but as of now, God has made no contact with Ka—the little girl."

Satan nodded. "That's good, Kid." The Devil patted him on the shoulder. "You're a good kid. Ain't computers great."

Satan walked away. "I wanna see you, Benny."

Satan methodically plucked one of his cigars from the humidor and lowered himself into his old recliner. Benny stood at his familiar spot in front of the coffee table. "Sit, sit," Satan said, motioning toward the couch. "You wear me out standin' there like a statue every time you come in here."

Benny cautiously hovered on the edge of the couch.

"So, can we trust the Kid's numbers?" Satan asked. He leaned back in his chair.

"Yes, sir," Benny said. "Without a doubt."

Satan punched the remote. A messy kitchen popped onto the life-size operations screen. "So how do we explain all this," Satan said, flicking a hand at the screen.

Benny recognized the Hart's kitchen.

Satan bit the tip off the cigar and spat it across the room. "She made me a cake," he said softly, preoccupied with the cigar.

"A cake, sir?"

"Yeah. A *devil's* food cake."

Benny snickered. "I'm sorry, sir, but I'm sure you can see the humor in that."

Satan cracked the faintest hint of a smile. "She was in that kitchen over three hours tryin' to get it right. Trashed the kitchen." He gestured toward the screen. "Finally got the icing on it, even put a little red devil with horns on it. Then she put it outside next to the snowman with a fork and a glass of milk."

"May I...see it, sir?" Benny coaxed.

Satan's mood grew sour. "No, you can't," he huffed. He punched the remote again and Katie's backyard appeared on the screen. A plate, a fork, a candle, and a tipped-over glass lay in the snow next to the snowman. "The dog ate it," he said.

Benny tried to crush a laugh that escaped in spite of him. "I'm sorry, sir." Benny composed himself, only to burst into another laugh when he glanced at Satan. "All right," his hand covered his mouth. "Not again, sir, I promise."

Satan waved off the comment. "No matter," he said. "I couldn't eat it anyway."

A long silence passed between them, Satan sucking on the cigar, Benny staring at the coffee table. "Is devil's food cake good?" Satan finally asked.

"Oh, yes sir. Excellent."

Satan nodded quiet acceptance.... He

suddenly rose from the chair. "Then we're not dealin' with God," he said.

"No, sir."

"Well, that's too bad," Satan said with a great sigh. Then he smiled. "I can't believe it." His head was down and his hands were in his pockets. "She actually wants to help the Devil—be my friend," he clarified. Satan stared at the empty plate on the screen.

"What is it, sir?" Benny asked.

Satan glared at Benny from the corners of his eyes. "That stupid little dog ate my cake."

"Yes, sir," Benny said. "We'll get him for that."

Satan nodded in defeated confirmation of the remark. "Nobody's ever baked me a cake before.... I want that dog."

Monday, December 16

Katie hummed *Frosty the Snowman* while she repositioned Snowman's nose. Satan could almost feel the soft little hands against his skin. He gazed into her bright blue eyes, eyes not unlike the ones he used to find comfort in such a long time ago—the eyes that would haunt his dreams forever....

"Hey, kid."

Katie took a quick step back. "Good morning," she said. "Are you Mr. Devil?"

"Yeah, that's right, I'm Mr. *Devil*," he said forcefully.

"Oh, Mr. Devil," she said, placing her little hands together. "I'm so glad you've come to visit!" Joy filled her little eyes. "I just knew you would. Did you like the cake? I couldn't think of anything you'd like, and I didn't know if it was your birthday or not and—"

Satan held up his hands and cut her off. "I didn't come to visit, and you're not listenin'," he shot back, "so shut up and pay attention. Like I was sayin' before I was so rudely interrupted, this prayer thing has gone a little too far, and it's time for you to knock it off and start bein' a kid."

She showed him a stern face. "That's not a very nice thing to say. After all, I'm only trying to help you."

"For one, I'm not a very nice person; two, I don't *need* your help. So, just knock it off. You understand me?"

"No, I don't," she said. "Why are you so mean to me?"

"You're not listenin'. I said—"

"I am listening, and I heard what you said," she replied indignantly. "You said you didn't come to visit, and that—"

"All right, all right, so you heard me. Now

look, I'm not here to answer a bunch of questions. I'm here to tell you you're playin' a dangerous game, and I'm not somebody you wanna be messin' with. You gotta knock it off."

"But I thought you'd be happy if—"

"Yeah, you thought. Well, maybe you're thinkin' about the wrong things," the Devil said. "You need to be thinkin' about Christmas and Santa Claus instead of thinkin' about the Devil."

"But I thought the cake would—"

"I didn't *get* the cake," Satan snapped. "Your stupid little dog ate the cake." There, he'd said it.

Katie lowered her head, and a long silence followed.

A disgusted sneer formed on Satan's face. "I didn't even get to smell it," he said.

Tears ran down her face and her mouth puckered up. "Freebie? Freebie ate your cake?"

"Oh, come on, now," Satan said. "Don't start that—"

"But it was your cake!"

"I know," Satan conceded.

"I baked it just for you!" She wept freely now.

"And it was a good cake," he offered quickly. "If it hadn't been such a good cake, he wouldn't have eaten it."

"I only...wanted to...do something nice for you! I didn't think about Freebie. I never know when you're going to be here, and I wanted it to be a surprise, and—"

"Well, it was," he said. "It was a nice—"

The realization struck Satan with crushing force. Suddenly the Universe came into sharp focus. Here was the most powerful demon in existence, the supreme Evil, standing before a weeping child with a real, honest-to...God emotion running wild in his head. And, no doubt, God was watching. If it was possible for Satan to feel such a thing, raw, uncontrollable fear cut through him.

Behold, I come as a thief....

The emotion raised its head from some dark, forgotten crevice in his broken life. But it would not bring him down, would not alter his agenda, and he would do what he had to do.

"—stupid thing to do," Satan corrected. The vision faded from his consciousness and the girl came into focus.

"I'm sorry!" Katie sniffed from behind her tears. "I was just trying to do the right thing!"

"Well, that's just it, kid. You don't know what you're doin' 'cause you're stupid. *You're* stupid, your little *dog* is stupid, and besides, I didn't want your old cake anyway. And I don't wanna be your friend, so get off my back. I got enough problems without havin' to put up with a stupid little kid followin' me around like a dog on a leash." Satan flung his cape around him. "Stay away from me, you little brat," he said, and vanished into the cold air.

"Please don't hate me!"

They were the last words he heard before he slipped through the dimensional wall and beyond her existence.

Benny stood at the main console in the Devil's lair cleaning up the Old Man's files, when the screen above him exploded in a blast of fire and smoke.

Benny fell away from the concussion and threw his arms up to block the heat from his face.

Satan emerged from the fireball, his eyes flashing, and flung his cape to the floor.

Benny rushed to pick it up.

"Get out!" Satan shouted.

"What's—"

"Get out!"

Satan stormed through the room. "Get *out*!"

"Yes, sir. Right now," Benny said, frantically gathering up Satan's cape. "Did you talk to Katie, sir?"

Satan whirled and roared a wall of fire toward Benny.

Benny blocked the heat storm with Satan's cape and stumbled backwards. "Yes, sir! I take it that means you did," he said. He dropped the cape and ran from the room.

Satan charged into the bathroom and twisted open the taps in his sink. Fire gushed from the faucets and boiled into a caldron. He plunged his hands into the flames and repeatedly flung Hell's fire into his face.

Breathing hard and deep, he braced himself on the sink, raised his head, and gazed into the mirror. In it, he saw the reflection of an old man, an old man who had just dropped his guard in the presence of his most feared enemy. Worse than that he saw the great Satan, the same great Satan who had just felt the terror of love in his heart for a child. He slapped himself across the face. "Get a hold on yourself, old man. You're slippin'," he said to the tormented face. "You can never allow that to happen again."

He rolled his eyes up, remained still, now acutely aware of some invisible force in his presence. "So you're not involved, huh? Your little pawn is acting on her own. Maybe." He bobbed his head from side to side. "Maybe not. We've played this game before, haven't we? I think you're pushin' my buttons. Testin' the fire. Maybe you have a new toy that no one knows about."

Satan studied his expression in the mirror, now severe and calculating. "If the little girl is one of your new toys, let me remind you: I used to break all of my toys, remember? And if you're not careful, *extremely* careful," he lifted his graying eyebrows and sneered, "I just might break this one."

Tuesday, December 17

"The dog is at the vet's office," Benny announced.

The group closed in around him to get the rundown on the plan. "They had a cyst removed from his leg and had to leave him overnight. That gives us tonight to get to the dog. So, I'm gonna send Miser in to do the job."

A cacophony of objections followed.

"Aw, no fair!"

"Miser always gets to do the good stuff—"

"Yeah."

"And that would be?" Benny said to his serial killer.

"Well...you know," Whacker said, scanning the faces around him for support. "Killing things."

Benny put his hands on his hips and shook his head. "That's the whole point, Whacker. That's why I'm in charge of this operation and you're not. Miser will give us the element of surprise, because he's a dog person. He has a way with them." Benny grinned. "You ever notice how dog owners often look like their dog?"

Snickers rose from the group.

"That's right," Benny said. "He looks like the dog."

Miser smiled and nodded appreciatively at this obvious compliment. "Gee, thanks Benny."

"Besides, this will give Miser an opportunity to grow, to show us he can do the tough jobs. Right, Miser?"

Apprehension clouded Miser's face.

Benny grabbed his shoulders and shook him, peering into his eyes. "Come on, you can do this thing. You used to work for a vet."

Miser's lower lip quivered. "Yeah, but I never had to kill a dog. I wouldn't even watch when they had to do it."

"But you know what to use, how much, where to find it; you're the only one who can do this. And those dogs will love you. You'll be able to slip right in there in the dead of night and take him down. You'll be the only one in the place, just you and all those dogs. And it's not like you've got to kill them all; you've only got to put one of them down."

Miser wasn't convinced.

Benny put his arm around the skinny man's shoulders. "And he's a *bad dog*, Miser. He used to bite me, and he's causing a lot of problems for the Old Man, and that's not good." Benny shook him. "You with me?"

Miser jerked his weasel head up in a show of courage and wiped the tears from his eyes. He nodded.

"Good," Benny cheered. He slapped Miser on the back. "The Old Man's gonna be proud of you."

Benny clapped his hands together sharply. "Okay, people, let's make it happen."

The group dispersed with eager anticipation and hovered around the Kid as he straddled the seat at his control terminal.

Miser took a seat at the console next to the Kid and closed his eyes.

"Don't worry," the Kid said. "I'll get you in and out of there without a scratch." His hands raked the keyboard. Miser disappeared into a blue haze that swarmed out of his console screen and engulfed him.

The raw animal smell was intoxicating. It brought tears to Miser's eyes. The Kid had dropped him in the back, in the stark white hallway between the treatment rooms. The Kid was good, and he was glad. The thought of being dropped into the reception area had terrified him. He had always broken into a sweat when he had to go out and hand someone an animal. But it was late, no one was here, and now that he knew he was safe the debilitating nervousness quickly burned away.

Every light in the place was on. Christmas decorations broke up the clinical atmosphere. A corkboard on the wall held photos of several dogs and cats dressed in funny-looking Christmas sweaters and hats. He stood there for a moment, checking them out, snickering occasionally. The door at the other end of the tunnel, the one with the wire-mesh window, would be the one that hid the cages. No one in there would have on a Christmas hat.

He slowly made his way down the hallway, looking for the supply closet, being careful not to make any noise. He walked past a suspension scale on his left and darted into a small alcove to his right next to a rack filled with glass bottles. There it was, a door with a red cross and a name on it: PHARMACY.

He silently twisted the knob and entered the shadowy room. He flipped the light switch and began his search. Where would it be? He scanned the shelves until he got confused then decided to start at the top and work his way down. He found it on the fourth shelf.

DANGER! SOCUMB POISON

His heart raced. He knew what it was but never liked to handle it, especially when the vet had sent him to get it. Now he would have to use it to kill one of his buddies....

He wiped the terrible thought from his mind and found a twenty-gauge hypodermic on a shelf behind him. The dog was small. Two CCs should do it, he thought. He drew up four, then carefully put the deadly poison back in its place.

Back in the hallway, Miser approached the kennel door and peered through the glass. The dim light in the room revealed a narrow corridor between two long rows of cages that climbed the walls. Nothing was moving. He could see the occasional tail or haunch against a wire cage door, its owner's body rhythmically rising and falling to the cadence of sleep. He placed his ear to the door. Nothing. He leaned against the door and slipped into the room.

Now the sweet odor of animal life overpowered him. He stood silent and listened, his brain cautiously searching for clues that would tell him someone was awake. He found none and tiptoed into the corridor with the death syringe in his hand.

His eyes scanned the cages. Freebie; that was the name to look for. There was Jake, and Fuzzy, Major Bill...Tuffy. He took a closer look at Tuffy. The dog couldn't have been over eight inches long. Plugger...Baby. Miser snickered. Baby must have weighed at least fifty pounds. Freebie....

Freebie? Was this his Freebie? He checked the spelling of the name. Yep, this was him. "Oh, wow," he whispered. "He *does* look like me."

He laid the syringe on the little lip of a shelf in front of the cage and checked the chart hanging on the door. Acepromazine had been administered late in the evening. The dog was out for a while and probably wouldn't know what hit him. Miser peered back into the cage. The little guy was sleeping peacefully. He didn't look very dangerous. He wondered why the Old Man was having such a hard time with him. But then, the Old Man had a hard time with everybody.

Miser eyed the little dog again and then checked the clock on the end wall. No need. He had all night. He at least had time to say a silent hello to all of his other buddies before he committed the evil crime. He would probably never be back here again anyway, so why shouldn't he?

He surveyed the cages behind him. He made his way down the bottom row, silently saying hello and goodbye as he went, and worked his way back to where he'd started. A huge black ball filled a cage on his right. The name on the door said "T-Rex." But it was the cage directly in front of him that caught his eye. The dog was unmistakable.

The strange odor pushed Freebie's heavy eyelids open. He'd been in here long enough for his brain to reset his baseline for recognizing new scents being introduced into his environment, and he picked up on it through the subconscious haze. It didn't appear to be a threat, nothing did right now. It was just new.

Movement. It was probably one of the humans who had been so good to him and given him some of that cold sweet stuff earlier. He could only see the backside of whatever it was. He inched his way toward the front of his cage, and something caught his attention.

Long and slender, the object lay on the little ledge beyond the wire in front of him. One end had a sliver of something that winked at him in the faint light when he moved his head about. He stuck his little paw between the wires and touched it. It moved. He touched it again and jerked the paw back. That wouldn't work. He curled his toes around the other end and turned the silvery sliver away from him.

A golden retriever! Happiness filled Miser's heart. He used to have a golden retriever named Buddy. He checked the name tag: Ranger. The dog was curled up next to the cage door, his nose against the wire. Miser reverently placed a palm against the wire. He felt the dog's hot breath on his hand. "Ranger," he whispered.

The dog opened his eyes and breathed a deep sigh.

"Hey, guy," Miser whispered. "Wow, you look like my old dog. You sure are pretty." He stuck a finger through the wire and touched the nose. "Yeah, nice dog."

The dog moaned.

"Yeah, I know." Miser couldn't contain himself. He chuckled, his voice rising as he stroked the moist nose, the finger through the wire no longer satisfying his paternal need to pet the beautiful animal.

The latch to the cage was on his right. With tears in his eyes he reached for it, lifted it, and it snapped up with a sharp click.

T-Rex ripped into his cage door in a vicious attack on the intruder.

Miser screamed.

He slammed Ranger's cage shut and shoved himself away from the terrifying black shape on his right.

A sharp sting pierced his hip when he hit the opposite wall of cages.

He screamed again and leaped away, throwing himself into the cage where T-Rex's teeth flashed into his face.

The kennel erupted into a wild screeching of terrified and confused animals.

Miser's hands shot out in front of him.

He spun between the walls like a cornered animal trying to protect its flanks, attempting to shush the enraged dogs.

Nothing worked, and something was wrong with his muscles. The room was fading into a dark tunnel. In a panic he stumbled toward the kennel door that was disappearing from his vision. He never made it. When the four CCs of Socumb hit him, Miser's eyes rolled back and his knees folded underneath him.

"Come on, Miser. Let's get it done," Benny coaxed nervously, looking over the Kid's shoulder. "Open the cage and get it done."

"Here he goes," the Kid said.

They watched Miser lay the syringe on the shelf.

"Now what's he doing," Benny barked.

"He's turning around."

"Oh, no."

"He's talking to the animals."

"And we can't reach him," Benny said.

"You got it," the Kid confirmed. "Wait. He's gonna pet one of 'em."

"Oh, hell," Benny moaned.

"Want me to pull him?"

"No," Benny snapped. "Let him work it."

"Look out," the Kid said. "He's gonna open that cage."

"No, Miser!" Benny yelled. "You stupid fool!"

"Don't do it, Miser!" the Kid shouted.

The screen detonated into Chaos.

"I'm bringin' him—"

"No!" Benny grabbed the Kid's shoulder. "Leave him—"

"He just poked himself in the ass with that needle!"

Benny smashed his fist into the Kid's cubicle wall.

"He's goin' down!"

"Pull him," Benny cried. "Get him outta there!"

The Kid made one keystroke, and Miser was on his way back to Hell before he ever hit the floor.

The intercom crackled to life.

Good work, guys.

10

Wednesday, December 18

It was 9:07 p.m., and Rusty (Spider) Toban sat motionless at his computer console in the muted light of his cubicle at GNG Headquarters. He was no closer than he'd been three hours ago to finding the Web page that would become the next feature in *The Spider's Web*. He had less than eleven hours before airtime to make that happen. That meant he'd be up all night searching for it, and writing the story after he found it—if he found it.

His nickname had stuck when an anchor-person claimed the reason he didn't have a life was because he spent his time crawling across the Web searching for electronic food. A life? Maybe not. A forty-one-foot sailboat, yes, and unique Web sites had made that possible. Consequently, he had officially named his Web site column on the GNG technology segment, *The Spider's Web*.

But tonight, no tantalizing sites had flown into the Spider's elusive net. After cruising approximately two thousand potential sites, none with any merit had surfaced.

He forced himself to pop the PAGEDOWN key, slumped back into his chair, and tried to rub the fatigue from his eyes. The Web was becoming a ghost town where skeletons walked the empty streets, a wasteland of electronic garbage, hate groups, raw sex, child molesters, perverts, idiots, zealots, and rip-offs. So much for the wonders of the information age.

He logged on to *coolsites.com*, his last chance to uncover the site that would put him on a roundtrip transatlantic cruise to the Canary Islands and back. He had spent the whole year planning the trip that would trace Columbus' voyage, and searching for the award-winning site that would make it possible. Four years in a row he had hung the award on his office wall and put the bonus in the bank. Now he was two weeks away from the end of the year, and the old saying about "all good things" floated behind his tired eyes as he plugged in the date and time for the last hour. Working backwards from the time he designated, his custom-designed search program would pull up every new site. The software was his genius. With it, he could find the latest Web sites within minutes of their coming on line.

The screen suddenly flashed and a message appeared under a group of listings headed: *WAYCOOLKIDS: DEC18: 2109:36 UPDATE PREPARING RECOVER MAPPING THROUGH WAYCOOLKIDS: PLEASE WAIT.*

Great, he thought. WayCoolKids was coming back on line after recovering from the mysterious crash that deep-sixed them two days ago. The screen began to scroll, and he hit the SEARCH key. When the screen changed and the data for the last three minutes formed, he praised his light-speed link to the T-3 dedicated line.

But the listings were the same personal sites common to most of the Web today. Everyone with an ISP account and an e-mail address could put up their own Web site. What a joke that had become. Everyone with a Web site was about the equivalent of everyone in the United States voting—it simply wouldn't work. The Net's routing tables were already approaching overload with no workable plan to prevent it. When *everyone* was on line and had a site, true chaos would rule.

When the search hit the m's, something caught his eye.

He stopped the search and scrolled back to

the previous page. The site, stuck between the other common individual name formats, read: *HTTP://www.mrdevil.waycoolkids.com.*

He sat staring at it. He checked the time: DEC17: 2111:36. The site had gone up just two minutes after the WayCoolKids restore was completed. His gut told him to check it out.

He clicked on the command line and typed the address. A Web page with a bright red smiley face in the upper left corner and a snowman in the upper right corner appeared. The snowman had horns. The header in the center of the screen read: "Please, help me save Mr. Devil."

He read, about the trouble in the world, about the Devil, God, scriptures from the Bible to support the argument...about the solution, and what he could do to help, even a short suggestion for a prayer: "God bless Mr. Devil." The close was simple and sincere: *Please, pray for Mr. Devil, so he won't be so mean and all the bad things in the world will stop happening.*

The page provided an e-mail address at the bottom of the screen.

He spun around to the computer on his left and logged on to WayCoolKids. He plugged in his GNG password, selected INSTANT CHAT on the main menu, and typed *angel@waycoolkids.com. Hi Angel. This is Spider. Are you out there tonight?*

While Katie read a message from Sugarplum, an INSTANT CHAT screen popped up with a message in it. The address was *spider@gng.com.* The short message read: *Hi, Angel. This is Spider. Are you out there tonight*? She told Sugarplum to wait a minute and typed, *Hi Spider. This is Angel.*

Toban waited...and waited, checked the clock, 2116:41. He'd give it another three—

Hi Spider. This is Angel.

His heart leaped. He pounded the keys. *Hello, Angel. I just visited your Web site. I'm a reporter with the Global News Group on TV, and I do a column on cool Web sites. Your site is definitely cool! I'm going to do a story on it, and I'd like to talk to you. Can I call you*?

His fingers rattled the keys, impatiently waiting for a response. Finally a message popped up. *I don't think so. You might be a bad person.*

He laughed and typed, *I understand. Please call GNG headquarters, collect, at this number, 202-466-6397, and ask for Randy Toban. Your call will be forwarded directly to me.*

He waited for the reply.

What does call collect mean?

He frowned at the screen and typed. *You don't know how to make a collect call*?

No, the response said. *I'm only eight years old.*

He sat staring at the screen. A smile formed. He would have to brush up on his Portuguese. He burst into a laugh and said, "God bless Mr. Devil."

11

Thursday, December 19

Benny quickly entered the Devil's lair.

"Sit," Satan snapped, jabbing a finger at the couch. "Come on, come on. I want you to watch this." He punched up the volume on his remote control.

Thank you, Doctor Roan. Dr. Jack Roan, our advisor on health and fitness. You can receive a copy of Dr. Roan's report on the critical importance of good nutrition and exercise from our Web site at www.gng.com.

Well, Randy Toban, our "Spider", thinks he's done it again. He has won the coveted "Next

Generation" award for his coverage of unique Web sites four years in a row, and he believes he's found this year's winner. We agree. We leave you tonight with...a devil of a story. Here's Randy with The Spider's Web, and a truly remarkable Web site.

Benny watched the details of Katie's Web site unfold on the screen and braced himself for the onslaught.

...claims that, if the Devil stops being mean, to put it in her words, "all the bad things in the world will stop happening." Think about that.

We called WayCoolKids to see if we could find our mysterious "Angel." They flatly refused to discuss it, saying they hold all information concerning their kids in the strictest of confidence, which should bring a sigh of relief to all you parents. Whoever she is, we know this about her. She told me she's only eight years old. Back to you, Richard.

Richard Atworthy turned away from the remote screen behind him. *All the bad things in the world will stop happening*, Atworthy repeated. He smiled into the camera. *Yes, and what a wonderful Christmas present that would be. Thank you, Spider.*

That's our report for this evening. Thank you for joining us. We look forward to seeing you again tomorrow. I'm Richard Atworthy in Washington. Goodnight from everyone at GNG news.

Benny didn't wait for Satan to respond. Katie was in enormous danger. He sprang off the couch. "We'll get right on it, sir. We'll do whatever we have to do to stop—"

Satan waved him off and crawled out of the chair, a little slower than usual Benny thought. "Nah. It's perfect," Satan said. Before he straightened up, he reached for his mauled cigar that lay on the coffee table . "It's like that guy on TV said. Think about it. So far, we got lots of kids prayin' for me, but we only got a handful of people at a dinky little church prayin' for the girl. What we need is lots of people, *millions* of people, prayin' for the girl, and very *few* people prayin' for the Devil. That makin' sense?"

Benny nodded cautiously, making sure he understood the logic "Uh, yes, sir. I'd say that's what we need."

"That way," Satan raised a finger, "God gets petitioned by millions of parents and other adults all across the world, intervenes on behalf of the girl, and breaks up this little pray-for-the-Devil club. Then all these stupid little kids stop prayin' for Uncle Satan, and we can all get back to livin' normal lives.

"Now, how do we get lots of people to start prayin' for the *girl*?" Satan spread his arms wide and threw Benny a knowing smile past the cigar clamped in his teeth. "We put her on TV!"

Satan waited, arms wide, cigar wiggling.

"Uh, Christmas might not be a good time to do that, sir. People are weaker and easily influenced during the holidays."

"Exactly!" Satan declared. He jerked the cigar out of his mouth. "You said it yourself. The Media is a powerful tool. We put her on TV, the world feels sorry for her, thinks she's possessed by the *mean old Devil*," he tried to look mean, "and starts prayin' for her. At that point, God has no choice but to step in and put an end to this nonsense or lose face in the eyes of His constituency." He shoved the cigar back into his mouth.

"With all due respect, sir, Katie's argument makes sense, and kids tend to do well on TV because they don't have a concept of the audience. It's possible that she could—"

"Are you crazy?" The cigar came out of Satan's mouth again. "Are you tellin' me the world might go for this pray-for-the-Devil business?"

"So far, we got two hundred thousand—"

"Yeah, yeah, I know, but those are kids." He flipped his hand at Benny and rounded the coffee table. "Adults know better than to pray for the Devil."

"Sir, lots of people worship you."

"Yeah, but they pray *to* me, not *for* me. The ones who pray to me are just a bunch of losers; they're not a threat."

Benny didn't ask why the others were a threat.

Satan raised his finger. "The adults will pray for the girl. Trust me." He shrugged. "After all, she's the one who's possessed, not me. She'll make a great scapegoat."

"Katie's parents will never let you put her on TV, sir."

Satan stuck the cigar back into his mouth and cracked a smile. "Of course not," he said, "but they'll let God do it, and I know just the person to make that happen."

Carrying a small plate of food, glass of water, fork, and napkin, Fred Frey had carefully made his way into the living room on his way to the couch and the evening news.

With the exception of Christmas, the room was just as his beloved Grace had left it, filled with the memories of their lives together with family and friends. Now, that family and those friends tried to get him to get out of the house every year and spend Christmas with them. And he did, but not this year, or last year...or the year before. Or they demanded they all get together at his place. This year they wouldn't, and he was glad. Such gatherings only made him miss her even more.

He now sat on the couch finishing up the last of his meager dinner, anticipating the light-hearted story at the end of the news that always followed the gruesome stuff. He understood why they did it that way—settle the nerves, all that. And he enjoyed watching the news while he ate dinner, but he often wished that someday he'd tune in and see nothing but good news.

He hadn't put up any Christmas decorations since Grace had passed on. She had loved Christmas, in the past, preparing for weeks for the annual pilgrimage that followed her invitations to the family. "They enjoy it," she would say as she spent days filling the house with her love in the form of little Christmas trinkets and toys and Santas and seemingly miles of lights and fake icicles and tree ornaments and such. Except for the lonely little eighteen-inch synthetic Christmas tree on the piano—the piano Grace would always play for everyone on Christmas Eve—the rest of the stuff was upstairs in boxes. Having lost its true meaning in today's world, Christmas was far too commercial for his tastes anyway, and that was a good enough excuse to not drag out the memories.

...believes he's found this year's winner. We agree. We leave you tonight with...a devil of a story. Here's Randy with The Spider's Web, and a truly remarkable Web site.

Reverend Frey swallowed hard the instant he

saw the little snowman with horns. He sat forward on the couch and placed his plate on the coffee table. The Web page on the screen belonged to Katie Hart. With every sentence that followed, every word that followed, his appetite grew weaker and the tightness in his chest grew stronger.

...claims that, if the Devil stops being mean, to put it in her words, "all the bad things in the world will stop happening." Think about that.

"Oh, my God. Have mercy."

...strictest of confidence, which should bring a sigh of relief to all you parents. Whoever she is, we know this about her. She told me she's only eight years old. Back to you, Richard.

The preacher hit the POWER button on the remote. The howling storm outside his windows filled the sudden void when the television winked out. The front of his shirt pulsed to the pounding of his heartbeat.

The situation was totally out of hand. Satan was on a campaign to align himself with the world's children, striking at the very core of the human race, its weakest point. Children praying *for* Satan today, praying *to* him tomorrow....

How extraordinarily clever of the Demon, Reverend Frey thought, ceaselessly searching for a new weakness in the spiritual fabric, a ruptured seam or minute tear where he might insert his influence and rip it open, spilling the souls of men into the streets of Hell. The appetite for such wickedness always escaped him, but its results did not. The world was infested with sin, the product of Satan's genius.

Dread filled his stomach. He returned the remains of his dinner to the kitchen, donned his heavy parka, and in spite of the weather stepped out onto his porch.

The night was a frozen hell, a hurricane of snow and ice. According to weather reports, it would take southeastern geography most of the night to subdue the blizzard's strength.

When he reached the sidewalk, he forced his eyes open and glanced up at the churning balls of fire he knew to be Christmas streetlights. A fierce north wind drove the sleet into his face like tacks thrown into the back of some immense atmospheric fan.

Only two blocks from his house, the church was invisible, concealed by the storm's fury. A dangerous storm, it could take his life in that short distance if he were to fall and break something. The perilous cold could kill him. No matter. God waited for him. He had to get to God's house. He ducked his head, leaned into the biting gale, and trudged on, his thoughts focused on his problem.

Yes. *His* problem. He'd been the one who planted the thought in the child's head. Now, she had a Web site with national exposure. He had underestimated Satan's tenacity—a foolish mistake. If ever he needed God's help to save this child, he needed it now.

He found the church and tromped up the steps. A wall of wind-blown snow covered the front of the building, molded by the wind like a painter's drop cloth. He kicked his way to the door, dug the knob out of the snow and jiggled his key into the frozen lock. He burst into the church and fell against the inside of the door to seal himself off from the storm.

Catching his breath, he shoved back the parka hood and brushed away the snow that had followed him in. The church was cold, shadowy, somehow forbidding. A frigid draft brushed across his neck and sent an icy shiver through his soul. Outside, the wind howled and lashed God's house with such force that it seemed the demons themselves were tearing at the stained-glass windows, seeking shelter from their own creation. He shook off the eerie feeling and flipped the light switch. The sanctuary glowed to life with the warmth of incandescent candlelight.

Reverend Frey made his way down the aisle and dropped to his knees at the altar. He placed his gloved hands on the oak rail, his attention on the figure of Christ on the Cross above him, and his mind on the story he had just seen on the national news about Katie's Web site. Had the situation been different he might have prayed at home, but the urgency of Katie Hart's problem warranted supplication at God's feet.

"Heavenly Father, I come to you on this wicked night with a heavy heart and unquestionable faith in your holy power, safe in the knowledge that you are the one, true God, the Creator, and the giver of all life.

"By my insignificant hand, a precious child has been led astray and wanders in the evil darkness of Satan's shadow."

"Yeah, you screwed it up Fred," Satan said.

He lounged on the pulpit banister with one leg cocked on the rail, his elbow resting on the knee, chin in hand, thoughtfully looking down on the pitiful minister. "But don't be so hard on yourself," he said, rising. "I got a plan that's gonna get us both out of trouble."

Fred continued his prayer while Satan paced and lectured.

I'm only one person—

"That's right," Satan confirmed. "You can't do it alone, and I don't expect you to. We need more people workin' on it, millions of people, all over the world, prayin' for your little friend." Satan stopped. "So we're gonna put her on TV."

Help me, Lord. Show me the way, that I might be...

The Devil raised his hand and continued to

walk. "Now, I know it'll humiliate her, but she's young; she'll get over it. Besides, she won't listen to reason, so we gotta do somethin' *big*," he threw an uppercut at the air.

"You gotta talk to the parents, Fred. Tell 'em this Web page business, that snowman, the cake, is all the work of the Devil. Tell 'em he's," Satan stopped and hung his head, then placed his hands together and shook his head while Fred rattled on, "tryin' to steal her innocent little soul."

...need a direction, to walk in your precious light...

Satan continued to pace. "That reporter wants to interview her, let her tell the world about her silly Web site. Think about it." He leaned on the rail. "That's exactly what we need.

"And this is a good time, Fred." He stopped in front of the preacher. "Christmas is all about love and all that nonsense. People feel like givin'," Satan was striding now, "doin' God's work. Everybody'll feel sorry for this poor little helpless child who's possessed by Satan," he made a possessing motion, "and rush to God's altar to save her from the Evil Demon!" He reflected on his speech and said, "I should've done this for a livin'.

"We'll even show some shots of the snowman in the back yard." He chuckled to himself. "When people see those horns they'll be furious. There'll never be another snowman built! People all over the world will be on their knees prayin' for this pitiful child. She'll be a major hit, and we need a homerun right now."

...me become a tool in your merciful hands, oh Lord.

Satan pointed a finger at the preacher. "Call that reporter in Washington and get him down here." He stopped at the lectern. He gazed at it momentarily then slowly—reverently—placed his hands on it, curling his fingers around its edges. "Our little angel is in serious danger, Reverend," he said softly. "She needs help, and I can't give it to her. God's gonna have to stop her. That's why you gotta force Him into action before it's too late. It's the only way we're gonna save her, Fred."

Satan released the lectern and disappeared into the chilled air.

Show me the way, oh mighty God, for I am lost without your light to mark my path. In God's holy name I pray...Amen....

Frey stood up and wiped his face. As was the case with most of his inspiring revelations, God's message was instantaneous, rendered with divine clarity.

That reporter in Washington wanted to interview Katie. He wanted to expose her to the world, let her tell her story, and Fred Frey needed an army to combat the evil that stalked the child. This was his chance to raise that army.

"Thank you, Jesus! Praise God almighty!" he shouted. He would call the Harts as soon as he got home. His next call would be to Washington, DC.

Wilma called Sam Boyle, the senior systems engineer for WayCoolKids Inc., at precisely 10:17:32 p.m. Sam thought the event odd. Aside from the mysterious system crash a week ago, she hadn't called him in months, and he had flinched when the buzzer in his pager announced her. While strolling down the hallway to the server room at WayCoolKids, he bumped into Art Kaplan, the second shift controller.

"Hey, what gives?" Art chuckled. "What're you doing in here at this hour of the night?"

"Wilma called," Sam said, sliding past Kaplan. "You know anything about that?"

"Not a clue," Kaplan said, shuffling papers into a series of open mailboxes aligned along a wall in the control center. "She was happy four hours ago."

Boyle entered the server room and slipped into the swivel chair in front of a computer screen. The message on the screen read: HELLO, SAM. I THINK WE HAVE A PROBLEM WITH STORAGE ALLOCATION! LOVE, WILMA. "Thank you, love," Sam said tenderly, his fingers popping the keys. "Let's see if we can figure out what's going on."

The powerful Web server that controlled the million-plus Web sites and e-mail addresses allocated to their customers, Wilma was the electronic brain inside WayCoolKids, Inc. In Sam's three years with the company, she had never failed them once, and her redundant automated auditing policies worked flawlessly.

Prowler, Wilma's system monitor that established, tracked and coordinated all of her system audit procedures popped onto the screen. Sam selected AUDIT TRACKER and the screen filled with a graph laced with colorful lines. The intense red one that towered above the others flared like an electronic fissure.

"Wow! What's going on here," Sam said. He clicked on the pulsing red line and another screen popped up, this one packed with scrolling rows of alphanumeric data that whizzed past him in a blurred fountain of information.

Suddenly the scrolling stopped. In the center of the screen, a single row of data highlighted in red jumped at him. He smiled. "Good job, Wilma." He clicked on the questionable record, and another graph appeared with real-time statistics running across the bottom of the screen. "What's all this about...?

"Art," Sam said to the door. "Get in here."

Kaplan entered the room. "What's up?"

"Traffic on this Web site, that's what's up," Boyle explained. "Look at this. Four hours ago this site had less than three hundred hits in the last twenty-four hours. Now look at it. That's a sixty degree line!"

Kaplan stared at the screen.

"And look at these percentage stats," Boyle said. "Seventy-two thousand seven hundred twenty-four hits in the last four hours." Boyle did the math in his head to double-check the figures. "Wilma's right. That's over a twenty-four thousand percent increase in the last four hours." He hit more keys. "Check this out. E-mail account for the same site."

"Wow!" Kaplan said. "Fifty-two thousand seven hundred thirty-six messages."

"Yeah," Boyle said. "In the last four hours, and it's still climbing. Let's see. Wilma's dumping to mailboxes every twenty minutes. That's," he did more math in his head, "over four thousand messages every twenty minutes. No wonder she's upset."

He went back to the Web site tracker. They both gazed at the escalating figures piling up at the bottom of the screen. "Good girl," Boyle said. "Look at that. Wilma has already brought the backup server on line and allocated secondary control of this site to it. When traffic peaks at ninety percent of her capacity she'll transfer control—"

"That's her!" Kaplan leaned on Sam's chair.

"What?" Sam said, frowning up at him.

"That's her!" Kaplan pointed to the glowing red record on Wilma's screen. "That's the site that was on the news earlier. *The Spider's Web* on GNG aired a story about this site. You'd already split when it came on."

Sam clicked on the domain name and Katie's Web site came to life before them.

"Yeah, that's it," Kaplan said. "This site's only been up for a little over a week, and this kid's only eight years old. Check it out."

Boyle read the site, then took his hands off the keys. "You're kidding." He made a deep sigh. "I'm gonna make Wilma happy and manually transfer this account to the Toby server before she hits memory meltdown on it. That should occur within," he glanced at his watch, "two hours." He shook his head. "One thing's for certain," he said. "From the looks of these numbers, I'd say *Angel* has hit on something."

...bless the Devil.... God bless Mr. Devil.... God, please save the Devil...Devil's soul and make him a better person.... God bless Mr. Devil...help the Devil be—

"No!"

Satan sprang up in the bed.

His mind screamed for relief. The room contracted and expanded in waves of psychological distortion.

He flung the covers back, grabbed his head, and fell back onto the bed.

"No! Stop!"

He rolled onto his right side, his left side. Spikes of pain shot through his body.

...God bless Mr. Devil.

He let out a fierce growl and swung his legs over the edge of the bed. The room flew around him, a whirling vortex of lost souls screaming in his head. He reached out to stop the spinning room and precariously rose to his feet. The momentum swept him into the ghostly carousel.

Consciousness slipped away.

He went down, helplessly spiraling, the bed rising above him. His hand reached out and struck the red button in the nightstand as he fell.

The only words that made any sense rushed from his mouth. "Help me, Benny!"

❧ 12 ❧

Friday, December 20

Reverend Frey met Katie and her parents in the lobby of the local GNG affiliate at 1 p.m. He shook Paul Hart's hand and hugged Rachael and Katie. "I know this all happened quickly, but it's God's will," he said. "Mr. Toban just got here. The airport reopened late this morning, and his flight landed about an hour ago." He looked down at Katie. "And he says he can't wait to meet you, my darling."

The studio door off the lobby opened and Randy Toban approached. He ignored the parents and the minister and knelt on the tile floor. "You must be Katie," he said.

He was a handsome man dressed in a solid blue shirt and gray pleated slacks, slender, dark wavy hair, good tan, and a snappy, pleasant voice. Katie liked him instantly. "Yes," she said. "And you must be Spider."

He laughed playfully. "Yeah, but you can call me Randy. Hey, we're going to have a good time today. You know what we're going to do?"

"Yes," Katie said. "You're going to talk to me about my Web site, and other people will get to watch it on TV."

Another laugh. "That's right," he said approvingly. "You and I will just sit and talk and have a lot of fun while the other people around us do their jobs. Later on, people at home will get to watch us on the news this evening."

He stood up and introduced himself to the Harts. "So, let's go into the studio where the crew is setting up. We'll meet everyone, and I'll show you how everything works." He offered his hand to Katie; she smiled and took it.

Inside the studio, Toban took Katie on a tour of the set.

"I know this was a difficult decision," Fred told the parents after the reporter led Katie away, "but it's best."

Rachael took his hand. "We appreciate everything you've done, Reverend. Maybe this will be the end of it."

"It will," the Reverend said. "Mr. Toban will get his story, and you'll get your little girl back. People all over the world will see what Satan has done. By tomorrow morning, millions of people will be praying for your little Katie."

Cocooned in his robe, Satan slouched in his dilapidated recliner, watching the evening news on GNG. His body draped over the chair like a weathered throw. His face was ashen, sunken, his eyes glassy and swollen with fatigue.

Benny had camped on the couch all night after finding the Old Man on the floor next to his bed. When asked what was wrong, Satan had managed to squeeze out the word "Nothin'." This morning he had sat in the old recliner for hours and done nothing but watch Ted Turner's buffalo wander around in the desert. Now he lay wilted, like a sick plant, on his ragged throne after a fitful night of delirious mumbling. It was obvious there would be no answer forthcoming, and the question of what was wrong hung thick in the air like a bad odor.

Even at the risk of torment in the Lake of Fire, Benny had checked the beer cooler next to Satan's chair. It was full, hadn't been touched. He also had checked the bar. Nothing touched there either. He had even run a dump on all encrypted priority transmission logs captured by the system audit. After five hours of filtering, decrypting, and analyzing data this morning, nothing explained why Satan had collapsed. Nothing explained why he now lay withered in the recliner, and no doctors had been summoned.... Odd.

Benny set a small table next to Satan's chair and placed the humidor on it. Satan made a feeble attempt to swat at him. "Will you stop hoverin' around here like a bunch of vultures or somethin'? You'd think I was dyin'."

"Yes, sir. I just thought you might want your cigars close to you."

"Well maybe I would," Satan barked, "but if I do I'll tell you. Now sit down. You're wearin' me out."

Benny retreated to the couch and observed Satan, drifting into and out of sleep during a GNG discussion on why world markets were making a comeback from a prolonged slump. Since early yesterday morning, Satan had not discussed any of his operations with Benny, he hadn't been seen in the control room, and the Kid was getting antsy about weak signals coming from the Old Man's data trunk. Unless he found a solution to this problem soon, all of their carefully planned operations would fall apart by next week. Benny cleared his throat.

Satan awoke. "Where are we on the Egyptian thing?"

He should know that, Benny thought. "It

looks good, sir." It didn't. "Mubundi is quickly establishing power in eastern Sudan," a lie, "and we expect Libyan aid to start flowing into the area any day...."

"So what else have we got?"

He couldn't stay focused on their operations. "Chuyang took your hint about that meeting with Chinese authorities and is still at large in the mountains. The Chinese have eased off on the rebels. They're concentrating their efforts on the Korean border for a while. The rebel unrest is spreading toward the food supply in the Chengu Basin in Sichuan Province. If we can starve a few million people we'll have a real mess over there." Benny and the Kid were trying to accomplish this behind his back, because Satan had not recognized the opportunity. And he wasn't following any of this report, Benny thought. He spoke up on the second nod. "Sir, do you want me to work on that virus in Ghana for a few days?"

Satan suddenly realized that he was nodding out and made a noticeable effort to regain his composure. He had forgotten that Benny was sitting on the couch, was even in the room. Now he knew that Benny was aware of his lapse in mental control. The realization drove him erect in the chair. How long? When had Benny entered the room?

Middle of the news? When the interview with Katie was about to air? Maybe five minutes. What had Benny asked him...? Africa. The virus. "No, no," he said, using a contrived display of restlessness to hide his attempt to visually verify his surroundings. "Everything's fine. I'll get back on that one in a day or two.

"Have we got the dog, yet?"

"Uh, no, sir," Benny said.

Satan snorted. "I can't believe it."

Benny looked away, then back at the Devil. "It's a smart dog, sir."

Satan managed to lift an eyebrow. "Oh yeah? Then maybe I oughta put the dog in charge."

...on our technology segment, The Spider's Web, Randy Toban profiled a devil of a Web site. The question—

"Ssssh. Here it comes," Satan said, now alert. He cranked up the volume on the remote.

...who the elusive "Angel" might be. Well, he found her. Here's the Spider with a remarkable story about an ANGEL who is trying to save the DEVIL.

"Good," Satan said, some of his strength returning. "Maybe we'll get some rest after this. You got the trackin' set up?"

"Yes, sir," Benny assured him. "The Kid's monitoring the Web site and her e-mail right now. We've also got all low-level broadcast signals under audit. We'll pick up any prayers that come through on her bandwidth, sir."

...extraordinary idea. Tell us how that happened.

They watched Katie explain how she got her idea to pray for the Devil from the preacher at her church.

"So Fred tells her to pray for those who persecute you, and she picks *me* outta the crowd," Satan said. "I've seen those idiots use the Bible to justify everything from snake handlin' to the Crusades, but I never thought I'd see this."

...that if Mr. Devil is the person causing all the trouble in the world, then he needs our help the most, so he's the one we should pray for, Katie was saying.

Toban flashed a conciliatory smile at the camera. *Now, you say you've talked to...Mr. Devil? That he becomes the snowman in your backyard? Tell us about that.*

"Oh, boy. Here comes the snowman bit. There'll be a worldwide public outcry after this one—oh, there he is. Look at those horns!" Satan laughed through a hacking cough. "I can just see snowman heads rollin' anywhere there's snow."

So, he's come to see you more than once? Toban asked.

Oh yes. Katie said. *Three times now. I think he's lonely, because he doesn't have any friends in Hell.*

"That'll do it," Satan said. "God'll be answerin' prayers twenty-four hours a day after that one. Good girl, Katie!"

Tell us about the cake, Katie, Toban said softly.

Silence....

Katie twisted her hands together.

"Oh, look at this," Satan said. He pushed himself forward in the chair. "Look at her clam up, and this guy's gonna just sit there and let her make a fool of herself while the world watches. Way to go, Spider!"

Katie wiped a tear from one eye. *I just wanted to do something nice for him*, she explained, *but I didn't do a very good job. He didn't like it, and my dog, Freebie, ate it.* She wiped her eyes again. *I tried to make it pretty, but I put the icing on while the cake was still too hot and...it melted, and it got all messy and...he told me he didn't want it, and....*

Toban studied his notes momentarily and appeared to be deciding whether to continue the interview or bail out. Katie was sniffling. The shot cut to Toban, to Katie, to a two-shot; back to Toban. Toban raised his head and said, *You know, Katie, some people say the Devil is trying to steal your soul, to make you a bad person like him.*

That's not true! Katie blurted without hesitation.

She began to cry.

No one wants to do anything for him. No one likes him. God doesn't even like him! I know I wouldn't be very happy if no one liked me. No one wants to give him a chance, or pray for him...or anything. No one even cares about him!

Well, I care about him, she said defiantly, *because I'm his friend, and I'm not going to give up on him. Jesus didn't give up on us, so I'm not going to give up on Mr. Devil, and I hope he has the very best Christmas ever....*

Satan didn't hear the last of the interview. Katie's declaration echoed in his head, snuffing out the ever-present roar of the Overlook. It also snuffed out any hope of saving her. The despair was almost unbearable. What was he going to do now? She wouldn't back down, and he *couldn't* back down....

The story ended without another shot of Katie, and somehow his finger pushed the POWER button on the remote. The screen winked out. An oppressive silence settled over the stone chamber.

"Sir, I'm sure all that's gonna play right into your hands if you give it time to—"

"Shut up."

Benny plopped his elbows on his knees and jammed his fingers into his hair. He suddenly rose from the couch and kicked the coffee table with a vicious blow.

Satan laid the remote on the little end table and sat slumped in the chair. “She defended me.” His weak chuckle rumbled in the crushing silence. “In front of the whole world, my little angel defended me.” Satan rubbed his face. “Oh, Katie, what have you done?” he pleaded with a great sigh. “You didn’t even tell ‘em I yelled at you.”

Benny spun around. “Sir, it’s obvious that Katie doesn’t mean any harm. She’s just a child,” he pleaded. “All these other people are trying to make what she’s doing seem—”

“Go away,” Satan said. He waved Benny out of the room. “Just go away.”

Benny marched over to the Kid’s console.

“Hey,” the Kid said. “How come you ran a dump on the system log for encrypted info? Something going on?”

“Shut up and bring all the boards up to date. I want to see all the low-level broadcast tracking audits, Web site tracers, Katie’s e-mail transmissions, and the Old Man’s bandwidth scanners, all in real time.”

The Kid wheeled around to his machine and whacked the keys. “You been in there all night and all day. What’s up?”

“Nothin’,” Benny said, echoing Satan’s terse explanation.

"Well, *something's* up," the Kid corrected. He pointed to the screen. "Look at the baseline activity on the Old Man's traffic. This was his baseline a month ago," pointing, "strong signal, lots of bandwidth action, normal for him."

The Kid relied heavily on baselines, snapshots of bandwidth activity taken at a given time, converted into graphic format, and used as a departure point for monitoring and analyzing signal strength. He had one on every operation and everyone who had anything to do with operations.

"Look at it today," the Kid challenged. He pressed a finger against the screen. "It's at the bottom of the scale, so weak I can't get a reading on it, just above the baseline. See? Three weeks ago I thought I might have had a glitch—when signal antenuation started. The Old Man's signal never gets weak," he clarified. "Now I've lowered the baseline twice in the last week. I know my systems," he said with authority. "That's no glitch; that's a trend."

The plummeting red line on the graph representing Satan confirmed his weakened condition, and Benny's observations that something was bad wrong.

"And check this out." The Kid hit more keys. "Baselines on his operations. Signal strength below every one of them."

Benny took a deep breath and exhaled. "Just

give me the data. I want dumps on all low-level broadcast signals every hour. Pull three of the guys off stationary ops and transfer the dumps to their consoles. I want reports routed to Satan's priority trunk throughout the night as long as we got data coming in."

The Kid's console beeped at him and a flashing alert pop-up screen appeared. "Then from the looks of this, I suggest you get ready for a long night."

"What?"

"We've got action," the Kid said.

Another screen appeared.

"We got data coming in."

DATA TRACK: ENCRYPT/INCOM:

#4-5683-967-52736/9/R/1WWH.

"This has gotta be a low-level broadcast transmission, and we've got six more right behind it."

MESSAGE: 93-9455-63837-FO7438.968.

"Yep," the Kid said. "There it is."

LV:PA10/IT1813:42HRS/ES....

"A live vector at priority alert ten, international transmission at twenty seconds ago, European sector. Ain't no doubt; those are prayers."

"All the way from Europe?"

"Yeah, and they're five hours later than EST. It's eleven o'clock over there."

Benny expelled a labored breath. "The Old

Man was right. People all over the world will be praying for Katie by morning."

"Wrong." The Kid sat motionless. "They're not for her."

"What?" Benny snapped.

"They're not for her," the Kid repeated. He pointed to his screen. "They're coming in on the Old Man's bandwidth. They're all for him."

The emergency alarm shook Hell's control center.

The night before, Sam Boyle had left two e-mail messages, two messages on the home recorder, and paged his boss once. Michael Stoecker answered the page within five minutes: Sam didn't page him without a good reason, and Stoecker knew that. After Sam's explanation of the events surrounding the surge of activity on the Hart Web site and e-mail service, the boss had said, "Don't panic. Let's ride it out until tomorrow." Well, they had ridden it out all day, the GNG interview with Katie Hart had aired an hour ago, and her Web page was taking hits like a spacecraft hurtling out of control through the Asteroid Belt. Now Sam Boyle sat in a chair in front of Stoecker's desk watching him go over the latest report on the numbers.

Michael Stoecker, the twenty-eight-year-old MIT honors graduate, CEO and sole owner of the internationally successful multi-million-dollar Way-CoolKids Inc., glanced at his watch.

"Those numbers are right off the wire," Boyle said, anticipating the question, "and have almost doubled since the interview. After this, bandwidth will have a whole new meaning for the Harts." Bandwidth was a measure of the amount of data flowing across Internet access lines, similar to water flowing through a pipe. Katie Hart's Web site was receiving information at about the capacity of the Mississippi River.

Stoecker studied the astronomical numbers before him. "You ever seen a site take off like this?" he said.

"Never."

Stoecker dropped the report onto his desk. "GNG called to get some information for their story on the girl's Web page. That's why I had you get the numbers for me earlier. They told me about the upcoming interview. Said they wanted us to know about it so we wouldn't be blind-sided by the aftermath. Did you see the interview?"

"Yeah."

"What do you think?" Stoecker probed.

"I think she's gonna need her own server by morning, and I think the parents are gonna have to go on welfare as soon as they get the bill for a month of T1 bandwidth."

"I mean about her idea," Stoecker clarified.

Boyle was nodding. "I think it's cool. Kid's got guts."

"Yeah, Randy Toban at GNG thinks it's cool, too," Stoecker said. "And that's good. Worldwide exposure on GNG gives us a lot of free publicity that would cost us thousands if we had to pay for it. Might be in our best interest to play along."

Boyle picked up on Stoecker's implication. "And it shows the world that we can handle disasters and still keep our kids safe, gives us a good reputation as stewards of the world's children."

"Demonstrates that we can handle surges in bandwidth."

"Yeah," Boyle agreed. "People all over the world praying for the Devil. Helps the little girl's cause, too."

"Shows the world that WayCoolKids isn't afraid of the Devil." Stoecker gave it a minute and said, "We ever find out what brought down the system?"

"Negative. We're still working on it."

To the point. Anyone less confident might have tried to worm their way out of that one. Total confidence in his judgement, regardless of the implications. Stoecker liked Sam Boyle.

"Eight-year-old girl starts praying for the Devil, puts her message on her little Web site, site explodes with activity. A day later, an entire computer system with tighter security and stronger firewalls than NORAD goes down, and the best engineer on the planet can't tell me what happened." Stoecker's pencil tapped the desk. "Could have been the work of the Devil," he said, his eyes still on the pencil. "What do you think about that?"

Boyle knew that his response to that question would determine the direction Michael Stoecker would take in this matter. If the system had gone down because of something Sam Boyle couldn't find, WayCoolKids and Sam Boyle's position were in serious trouble; if the system had gone down because of the Devil—whatever that meant—everyone was off the hook. Sam had checked everything inside the firewalls, and he was certain that WayCoolKids was secure. The problem lay beyond their protective screens in the world of high-speed WAN technologies that connected them to the world, and Sam Boyle would find the problem, Devil or not. He spoke and never broke eye contact. "I don't think anyone but the Devil could slip something like this past me."

Correct answer. "I don't either," Stoecker said. "That's why I pay you six figures a year."

Stoecker considered the situation while he studied the framed photograph of his one-year-old daughter that occupied the right corner of his desk. She sat on a blanket with a little stuffed lamb pinned to her chest, leaning forward, her head tilted back, all teeth. They had given her the lamb just thirty seconds before the shot, and he could still hear the little yips of joy every time he looked at the picture.

He popped his pencil down on the smoked-glass desktop and stood, turned to the glass wall behind him that faced west across the desert peaks of the ancient volcanoes beyond Petroglyph National Monument in Albuquerque, New Mexico. "Set her up with her own server on a dedicated Fractional T1 line and scale it up as needed. Since it appears that someone is on to us, I want tighter physical security at all of our sites. I'll let GNG know what we're doing. We won't worry about the money. Let's just have a good time with this and see where it goes."

It was none of Boyle's business, but he asked the question anyway. After all, he'd been watching the numbers rise like raging floodwater. "Have you spoken with the parents, told them the deal, what kind of money they're looking at?"

"Yes," Stoecker said.

"What'd you tell them?"

Stoecker smiled. "I told them they weren't looking at any money, and then I said Merry Christmas."

Boyle slapped his hands together. "I knew you'd do that."

Satan stood next to the chair, slumped over, the fingers of both hands clamped to the chair arm. Weakness flashed through his body like a firestorm.

He had to move, get to the bed.

He let go of the chair and attempted to move the right leg forward. No strength.

He went down, tumbling like a shot animal, and took the small table next to his chair with him. He crashed to the floor.

Voices.... "*Benny*? Is that you, Benny?"

Benny burst into the chamber.

Satan crouched on the floor on his hands and knees, immobile in a graveyard of broken cigars.

"I'm here, sir!" Benny ignored the cigars and dropped to his knees. "What's wrong? Can you tell me what's wrong?" Satan collapsed on his side in a fetal position and groaned.

Benny grabbed him under his arms, dragged him into the bedroom, and laid him on the bed. "What's going on, sir? Tell me what's wrong so I can do something."

"There's nothin'...you can do." Satan sucked in heaving breaths. "It'll pass."

"Why don't we get the doctors up here?"

Satan recklessly swung his head from side to side. "Doctors can't...do anything...have no power," he said, every breath now a struggle. "I'll be...all right." He tried to rise up and fell back onto the pillow. "We have to...get the China thing straightened out."

"I'm taking care of that, sir."

"That virus—"

"We're on top of that too, sir. Everything's fine. We got the boards covered, and all your ops are running auto til we figure out what's going on."

Satan seemed to hear and accept that and gave in to whatever force had him lying helpless on the bed.

Benny sat on the edge of the bed. "Sir, can I get you anything? Is there something you need? If there's anything the boys and I can do, I'll get them on it right—"

"I've got to talk to Katie," Satan said in a gush of breath. He smiled weakly. "Got to see her. She comes outside...every mornin'...to see...if I'm there."

Benny forced a smile. "Yes, sir. I know."

Satan collapsed again. "I have to see her," he whispered. "Got to stop her."

Benny placed his ear close to Satan's mouth in an attempt to catch the escaping words.

"...to stop...it's...late...late...." Those were the last words he spoke. Satan closed his unfocused eyes and plummeted into a comatose sleep.

Benny slipped out of the room and pulled the door shut. He wandered into the main chamber and stood with his hands in his pockets, his eyes fixed on the aftermath of Satan's collapse, while the Overlook flickered like some colossal crimson flare in the night. He scooped up the remains of the cigars and placed them back in the humidor, then went back to Satan's bedroom. He set the humidor on the nightstand, took a brief look at the ghostly figure on the bed, and returned to the main chamber.

Unable to formulate an explanation for Satan's decline, he walked back through the logic of the situation while he paced. The Old Man had lost control, and that wasn't supposed to happen—*couldn't* happen. Could it? Had this ever happened before? No one had ever spoken of such a thing. Of course Satan was...how old? Well, how old was the universe? Who would know? Maybe God knew something, but Benny couldn't talk to God and had no desire to do so.

It'll pass. He turned the phrase over in his mind. Satan knew what was wrong. If he knew what was wrong it had apparently happened before. If it had happened before, he had survived it because he was still here, so he'd probably make it this time.

It'll pass.

Unacceptable.

Benny's attorney instincts told him to take nothing for granted. Information, that's what he needed. Suddenly, he stopped. Satan's old chest, the one that Benny knew held the diary Satan had told him about, commanded his attention as if it had spoken to him. *Everything anybody ever wanted to know about God, Heaven, Hell, the nature of Creation and Time...me, is recorded in the pages of this diary. I wrote down everything.*

Research. Quality research had brought down many of his opponents over the years. And like any powerful tool, good research required commitment, tenacity, and often, great risks.

Everything?

The thought drove him to kneel cautiously in front of the gold-laden trunk. Pandora's box, he thought. What terrible things lay hidden within? Things he was forbidden to see. Things that would perhaps wring a scream out of him and bring Satan out of his coma to cast him into the fire. Need-to-know applied not only to the FBI, it made life in Hell easier as well.

Benny had never touched the diary, knew it was off-limits, didn't want to touch it now. Perhaps demons lurked inside the mysterious chest. On the other hand, perhaps the forbidden diary's pages explained Satan's condition. He needed to know, now. He held his breath and slowly opened the heavy lid.

The diary lay on the bottom of the chest, all alone, a black mamba curled in its nest. Did he dare touch it? So far, he felt nothing, sensed nothing.... His hand descended into the darkness and retrieved the artifact.

It was just as the Old Man had described it, heavy, its cover soft as goose down, made of some silky fabric finely woven with what appeared to be gold thread. Some kind of pattern within its weave loomed beyond his comprehension as he angled it to reflect Hell's fire.

He carefully opened the diary to the first page. The words, written in a delicate gold script, seemed uncharacteristic of the mind that had formed them. This was a different mind, a mind Benny had never known.

"Oh, man. This is incredible." He glanced around as the whisper escaped his lips. With time screaming into his ear, he moved to the dining table, sat down, and began to read.

13

Saturday, December 21

The sound snapped Satan's eyes open.

"Katie?"

He found himself lying in his bed, weak and disoriented.

"Katie!"

Her voice. She was in the backyard, talking to Snowman, talking to *him*. Now would be his only chance to reach her.

"I'm comin', Katie. Don't leave me!"

His strength slipping away, he dragged himself off the bed and fell onto the floor.

Mr. Devil? *Are you there*?

He struggled to his knees, weakness coiled around him like a great serpent, the demon within him being awakened.

"Katie!"

Time. There was no time. His empire was threatened, and the demon would answer the call to save him as it had throughout eternity, swiftly and without conscience. He rose up, stumbling toward the door and into the main chamber where he went down again, taking a dining room chair with him.

He lay on his back, the main control screen looming above him. Katie stared down at him, the seconds slipping away, until finally, she would turn and go into the house, and it would all end before he could stop it.

Just a few more steps and he'd be at the main console where he could initiate transport to her. He rolled over, pressed himself into an unsteady crouch, and plowed into the main control center like he'd been shot in the back.

He collapsed onto the console and fell backwards into the chair. His fingers raked at whatever he could reach, dragging an array of equipment into his lap.

He dug the keyboard from the pile and hit the LOCKOUT key that severed his connection to Hell's control center. His head fell back, his eyes now barely able to focus on the fading screen. Katie was saying goodbye.

"No!" he cried and began hitting keys.

"I have to see you before—"

The screen flashed blue.

"—it's too late!"

The keyboard tumbled from his lap.

With the room fading from his view, he made a stab at the transport switch. The alarm sounded.

He fell limp onto the console, and the blue mist swept him away.

Satan crashed into the snowman.

She was disappearing.

Stop her, you fool! "Katie! Katie, stop!"

"Oh, Mr. Devil! Is that you?" She ran back to the snowman, did a little hop and clapped her hands. "I'm so happy to see you. I didn't think you were coming." She frowned up at him then took a step back and peered into the eyes. They were sad, lonely, filled with pain. "You should be happy. Are you still mad about your cake?"

Satan frantically shook his head and caught his breath, straining to push the words out. "No. I'm sick, Katie, and I need...your help."

"Perhaps you've caught a bad cold." She couldn't cure a cold, but maybe she could cheer him up. "Well, you'll feel much better after you hear the good news." She put her little hands together again. "People all over the world are *praying* for you. Isn't that wonderful!"

Satan clung to the snowman, his strength melting away. "I don't have...much time, so...you gotta listen to me."

Satan's weak, raspy voice struck a sense of urgency in her. It wasn't a cold. Hell was probably too hot for anyone there to catch a cold, and snowmen didn't catch colds. "I think you should see a doctor," she said. "Do you have doctors in Hell?"

"Doctors can't help," Satan said. "You...are the only one who can help me."

"Me?" she said, and then she smiled. "Oh, I know. I'll go to the Web site and tell everyone you're sick, and maybe even more people will start praying for you, and—"

"That won't work." Satan shook his head violently. "You gotta *stop* prayin' for me! You gotta tell everybody...you made up the whole thing. Tell them I'm not the snowman. Tell them...you're possessed by the Devil."

"But that's not true!"

"And you need God to protect you from me."

"No!"

"Yes!" Satan said with all the force he could pull together. "You're in serious danger. You need God's help."

"But what about you? You're sick. I want to help you."

"No!"

The demon awoke.

"Don't you understand!" he roared. His words escaped past its teeth. "Run!"

Katie threw her hands to her face and screamed as she turned away.

"Run, Katie! Run!"

Weakened to the point of collapse, he could no longer overpower the thing that made him what he was, his true guardian, the force that would save him, the demon that would destroy everything that threatened him and the empire, even his precious Katie. Time had run out.

He opened his eyes, or so he thought. He couldn't be sure. She was slipping away, into the abyss that would consume her. He spoke the last words he knew he would ever say to her.

"I love you, Katie. Please forgive me."

Sunday, December 22

Benny paced from one console to another, wiping sweat from his face, giving orders and attempting to track the latest events that cluttered the main board in the control room. All current operations were running in active red-alert status, and data was streaming in from around the world like lava flows from a raging volcano.

"What's up, Miser?" Benny stood over the little man. Sweat dripped off his chin onto Miser's shoulder.

Miser glanced up. "We got rebels on the run in the western provinces of China."

"What?" Benny declared. "I thought we had that sector tied up a few days ago."

"Yeah," Miser said, "but Chinese forces shifted their focus to that border this morning. With India on the warpath, the rebels have pulled out of the region claiming it's not worth the losses they might suffer."

"Work on it," Benny said. "Try to draw the rebels into a fire fight and spill it across India's borders. I want India in on this before tomorrow. We can't afford to lose China.

"Hey, Kid," Benny yelled. "I need that status report three minutes ago."

"Okay, okay, here it comes," the Kid replied.

Benny swooped down on the boy. "How's it looking?"

"We're forty-eight hours in since Katie's story aired, and we've got a global response now, most of it coming from the major metropolitan areas of the world—that's where the computers are. Looks like we'll be up all night again."

The Kid changed screens and shook his head.

"I don't get it," he said. "Just three days ago the Old Man had North and South Korea ready to slit each other's throats, and now they're gonna sit down and talk tomorrow.

"And we've got serious problems in North Africa tonight. Egypt laid down the law to Libya. Libya's backing off. The rebels in the Sudan failed to topple our warlord in the eastern section. If they lose that area, the threat of intervention on the part of Egypt will be lessened. Once the rebels pull out, Egypt will come off the throttle. No more war."

"Get on it. I want Libyan terrorists on the ground in Egypt. Let the rebels know that. Libya cannot drop their support for the rebels. If they show signs of weakness, it's all over.

"What about the viral outbreak in Ghana?" Benny said. He punched a finger at the Kid's screen. "I want a full report on that virus ASAP. The Old Man's got too much work in that project. We can't afford to lose it."

"Here we go with the news," the Kid said. He hit some keys and transferred the image at his console to the main control room screen. Music came up under the words.

In tonight's news, the rebels in China are pulling back; the source of a killer virus discovered in Ghana has been found; Libya is backing down in the Sudan conflict; the demilitarized zone between North and South Korea is quiet tonight, and an eight-year-old girl is trying to change the world.

The news anchorperson appeared on the screen.

Good evening. I'm Richard Atworthy in Washington. Our top story tonight centers on little Katie Hart, the eight-year-old girl who decided that the way to solve the world's problems was to pray for the Devil. She put up a Web site to encourage others to do the same, and since we interviewed her last night, the eight-year-old has become the poster-child for a worldwide movement to save the Devil that is burning out of control. We begin tonight with Joe Hendrick in Atlanta, Georgia where a child and her dream were born. Joe?

Thank you, Richard. We have learned that four hours after our interview, WayCoolKids, Inc., the Internet Service Provider who handles Katie's account, set up special servers just to handle Katie's e-mail. At this hour, her Web site has taken—get this—372,654,483 hits, and she has received more than 261,000,000 e-mail messages. WayCoolKids is so taken by the attention she has received, the president of the company says they will not charge her for the additional services needed to handle this extraordinary event.

And this seems to be only the beginning. It appears that people all over the world are following Katie's lead and PRAYING for the Devil's salvation. Could this be the beginning of an unprecedented event in human history?

Benny and the rest of the crew gathered around the Kid's console and watched the story unfold on the screen.

GNG and the three local news affiliates had the Hart's house under heavy surveillance on a twenty-four-hour rotation schedule. Brightly-colored live-feed vans and other vehicles with microwave antennas aimed toward the sky lined the highway that bordered the Hart's large front yard. Other smaller stations and a host of newsprint and national magazine reporters lingered throughout the day and night. They would remain for as long as the money and the frigid air would allow.

The police had been called, not by the Harts, but by motorists who had complained about the congestion. Under police direction, it was either move the vehicles off the shoulder of the road, or move along. The seasoned news hounds had simply straddled the ditch that bordered the Hart's property with their vehicles. As far as they were concerned, highway easements were designed for that purpose.

Now, as a precautionary measure after having removed two of the news crews from the property line fence that separated the Hart's backyard from their neighbors, the Atlanta Police Department had a cruiser stationed at either end of the media carnival. Determined to get shots of "Mr. Devil" as Katie's snowman had come to be known in the media blitz, the news organizations promptly called in their choppers to hover over the house like birds of prey. This action led the police to call in their choppers to break up the operation.

Everything was falling apart.

"Miser," Benny said quietly, "I want her Web site brought down immediately."

"But this is the Old Man's operation."

"Shut up and do what I say, or you'll find yourself on the other side of the Overlook. Now get it done! Bring the whole damn system down if you have to.

"Pusher," Benny turned to the man at the next console, "find our zealots and have them call in bomb threats to WayCoolKids. Have them tell WayCoolKids that if they don't remove Katie's Web site from their servers, they'll pay for it. Better still, I want someone to blow up one of their satellite locations before the warning is issued, just to remove any doubt from their minds.

"All right, break it up. Let's get to work. I want all of our current operations in priority alert until further notice," he said to the room. "Let's make it happen.

"Kid, I want every prominent televangelist in the world on the news and the talk shows screaming about devil worship, social and moral collapse—all that stuff. Get one of those GNG news crews over to Frey's house. I want updates routed to the Old Man's control center every hour."

Benny headed for the Devil's lair.

The Kid caught up with him at the door and grabbed his arm. "Hey, what's up, Benny," he whispered. He glanced over his shoulder. "What's the deal with the Old Man? All his operations have lost their strength. The China thing is going under. He's all but lost the African virus. The Korean conflict will be over in less than a week unless he gets on it. The Libyan campaign's on the blink. And he's cut himself off from the main board. I can't even get tracking on his signals anymore. We haven't seen him in three days. The crew's getting edgy. And now you're taking over his ops. What's going on?"

"Look, do your job, keep your mouth shut, and don't worry about the Old Man's operations," Benny said.

"But the boards! His signal is so weak I can't track it anymore. I gotta keep his boards in sync with all the other operations so I can coordinate mission activity, and I can't do that without a track on his signal. It's like he doesn't exist any—"

Benny clamped his hand over the Kid's mouth. "Shut up! We got enough problems as it is without the crew overhearing anything that'll put questions in their heads, understand?"

The Kid nodded.

"So, you need to know what's going on?"

The Kid nodded behind Benny's hand.

"Okay, take short breaths til you get used to the air."

"Oh, no! In there?"

Benny shoved him into the Devil's lair.

The Kid doubled over into a knot, grabbed his chest, and gasped for air as the door shut behind them. "My God! It's hotter than hell in here!"

Benny grabbed him by the collar and led him through the main chamber. "You know that air-conditioning I told you about?" he said as the Kid stumbled along. "It went down yesterday. Now, shut up, and pay attention."

Benny stopped at the door to Satan's bedroom and jerked him upright. "You keep your mouth shut about what I'm gonna show you, or you'll find yourself on the other side of the Overlook, too. You understand me?"

"Yeah, sure, anything. Let's just get this over with." When they entered the Devil's bedroom, the Kid lost all concern for his roasting lungs.

Satan lay motionless on his bed, his arms at his sides, his body covered with a glowing veil of ethereal flames.

"Oh, my God!" the Kid whispered.

Benny shoved him back out of the room.

"Is that really the Old Man in there?"

"Yeah, that's him," Benny said, leading him away from the door and into the main chamber.

"But what's wrong with him? He looks—"

"I don't *know* what's wrong with him," Benny said, running his hand through his hair. "I've been trying to figure that out." They stopped next to the ornate dining table and Benny's fingers fidgeted with its edge. "He's been that way all day. He's been unconscious now for about three hours."

"What? No wonder I can't get a signal on him! What's going on here?"

"I don't *know* what's going on," Benny snapped. He sank into one of the chairs at the dining table and rested his face in his hands. "I just know the Old Man's in trouble, and I don't know what to do...."

The Kid dropped into a chair, reached across the table and gripped Benny's arm. "Let him go, Benny."

Benny's head jerked up.

Kid shook the arm. "Think about it. If he dies, maybe everything changes and we—can he die?"

"Of course not," Benny said. "Satan can't die. He's immortal...I guess." He dashed that thought and said, "Anyway, forget it. The Old Man's been good to us," he held up a finger, "and *you* think about it. He's a lame duck, like a President. He's been there, done it all. It's a job, and he's lost interest. If something happens to him, and we get some hot-headed young demon in here who wants to reinvent the wheel and conquer the world, we'll all be swimming in the Lake. As long as we got him," he jerked a thumb over his shoulder, "we got it made, so you keep that in mind. Besides," he added, "the Old Man's not such a bad person—devil—once you get past the politics." Benny picked up the diary. "He's even a poet."

"The Old Man? A poet? Get outta here."

"See this?" Benny held the book so the Kid could see the cover. "It's his diary."

"No way!"

"Yeah," Benny said.

"Wow! I wouldn't have thought the Old Man kept a diary."

"No one else would've either," Benny said. He shoved a finger at the Kid's face. "So you keep your mouth shut. It's no one else's business." Certain he'd gotten his point across he said, "I've been reading it. I thought if he'd been sick before, there might be something in here about what to do for him. Just my luck. He's never been sick a day in all eternity."

A reverent silence followed as his hands rubbed the ancient relic. "This is his only valuable possession." Benny gently thumbed the pages and snickered. "He managed to smuggle it out of Heaven when God kicked his belligerent ass out."

"No way."

"Yeah," Benny said. "It's a day-to-day history of his life in Heaven from early childhood." He stopped at a page and paused for a moment. "Seems strange," he said. "This is a side of the Old Man we never see, and never heard about when we were alive. He talks about walking along the River of Life as a child, holding God's hand," he chuckled, "questioning everything in his path. About playing in the many gardens and palaces with his friends. He wrote down everything, including what God knows. There's even a map of Heaven in here."

"No way!"

Benny held the diary open and showed him the map.

"Oh, wow! Man! That's cool!"

Benny thumbed through the diary again. "Here," he said. "Read this page." Benny handed him the book.

The Kid hesitated to touch it.

"It's all right," Benny said. "I read all of it last night."

The Kid wasn't convinced.

"Oh, go ahead," Benny chided. "What's he gonna do, send you to Hell?"

They both got a little laugh out of that one,

and the Kid took the diary. He read, then stopped in mid-sentence and started over, reading aloud:

" 'My Precious, Sweet, Eternal Love, Heaven's True Flower, The Song My Heart Sings. Bound As I Am By My Station To Do So, Love Beyond You, Sweet Love, I Cannot. You Are My Sea, My Sail...My Journey. My First, My Last, My Every Thought, Breath...And Dream.'

"Wow, cool! The Old Man wrote this?"

Benny nodded. "Yeah, to another angel."

"He was in love?"

Benny nodded again.

"That's awesome!"

Benny sighed heavily. "I guess," he said. "He paid a terrible price for it. God broke it up, and the Old Man never recovered."

"Why did God do that?"

Benny cocked up an eyebrow. "Have you ever read the Bible?"

The Kid appeared hurt.

"Sorry," Benny said. "Don't feel bad. I only read it when I wanted to use it in court to play on someone's emotions. Satan was created to glorify God, and God is a jealous God....

"They knew each other as kids," he went on after a moment of reflection. "We don't even know her name, but we know Satan fell for her. Loved her more than he did God. That was a bad mistake," he said. "Look at the next page."

The Kid flipped the page. The words were suddenly a dark, blackish crimson and wild in form, devoid of the beautiful gold script that graced the previous pages. "What happened. It's—"

"Blood," Benny said. "You ever notice that pointed fingernail on his left forefinger?"

"The one that caused that hole in the side of your neck?"

Benny chuckled and unconsciously felt for the hole. "Yeah," he said. "The diary says that when God split them up, Satan sharpened that fingernail. Every night after that, he'd prick the tip of that finger and use the fingernail to make entries in the diary in his own blood."

Benny shrugged and sighed. "Everything went to hell from there. He wrote the last page the night before God exiled him. He never wrote in it again. Seems that everything good in him had died by then, and he never got over the girl—angel."

"Hey!" the Kid said. "This thing's worth a fortune! And if what God knows is written in here, and somebody on the outside ever got their hands on it...wow!"

"Yeah," Benny said. Hell's noticeably dim flicker from the Overlook played across the side of the Kid's face. It grew weaker by the hour, a dying campfire at an abandoned outpost. He reached for the diary. “You keep your new perspective on the Old Man in mind once you leave this room, but don’t ever underestimate his power.” Benny pushed away from the table. “Now, we’re gonna go out there and get the job done, ‘cause he needs our help, and you’re gonna keep a nice, straight face until whatever this is blows over.”

Satan walked along a colonnade of angels, their wings slowly fanning the multitude of guests who lined each side of his route and stretched into the distance. Bouquets sprouted from their hair and rose in fanning arches above him, stippling God’s light on this beautiful morning.

A kaleidoscope of flowers covered the walkway under his bare feet. Petals rained down upon him as he made his way toward the majestic, open gazebo at the end of the colonnade, itself framed by Heaven’s light that flowed between its columns like rivers of gold.

Friends waved to him from the crowd, friends he hadn’t seen for an eternity. They cheered and clapped their hands, their faces luminescent with love. He waved as he walked, smiling, touching a hand here and there as he passed by. How good it was to finally be home! He had waited so long, and now it was over. The pain, the isolation, his endless, horrid existence, now nothing more than a haunting memory that faded with each toss of a flower, each sparkle of an eye.

When he reached the gazebo, he stopped at the foot of its steps and gazed up at the throne. God stood at its center in all of His glory, surrounded by angels and pillars of light. He recognized Gabriel at the left hand of God.

God approached and embraced him, then held him at arm's length. He waved to his right and music sounded, announcing another arrival. Satan faced the colonnade. The assembly cheered, and Satan stood transfixed.

She skipped and danced along the colonnade, radiant, beautiful beyond description, her streaming hair woven with flowers and gold ribbon. God's light surrounded her. A host of angels danced, played, and fluttered about her. She stopped when she reached him and offered him her hands.

His precious Mariah.

How he had missed her, dreamed of her, longed for her...wept for her, and now she stood before him with God's blessing.

Satan threw a questioning glance over his shoulder.

God nodded.

Was it possible that he would once again hold those tender hands, feel them against his skin? Did he dare touch her, show his eternal love for her in God's presence? He took her hands and slowly pulled her to him, held her, kissed her, and the music stopped.

The demon within him reared up and consumed her with fire.

"No! Leave her alone!"

The dream had awakened him.

"I'll stop her!" Satan screamed, his eyes wide with fright.

The protest came too late. The demon rose from the bed, lifted its ugly head, and bellowed a firestorm at God that torched the room.

The Beast stood in the flames, its breathing heavy, each exhausted breath a gush of fire. "Look what you have done," it cried, its ghoulish arms thrust upward. "Is there no peace with you? Is it not enough that I have been exiled and tormented because of your petty jealousy? Must it now come to this?" The demon roared another blast of fire and charged into the main control room.

"You have always taken away," it lumbered violently through the room, raking whiskey bottles from the bar, tearing at whatever happened to be in its path, "everything...I have ever loved! Must you take this from me as well?" the Beast cried.

"You dare to come after me hiding behind a helpless child!" It swept the array of electronics at the main console into a shrapnel explosion. "You spineless coward! Do you not have the courage to face me?"

It lurched to a stop and howled with all its strength, gnarled fingers curled into ghastly fists and shoved into the air. "Then so be it! If this is how it must be, then I will *show* you what I will do! I am the great Satan!" it bellowed with emphasis on each word. Fists pounded its chest. "I will *never* be brought down! If you must have her, then I shall deliver her to you!"

With its shoulders slumped in defeat, the demon bowed its head. "I shall deliver my Katie to you."

14

Monday, December 23

"Yes!" Benny snapped.

It was ingenious, a perfect setup. Freebie was in the back yard, no one was around, and the truck was coming right past Katie's house. Here was a chance to fix at least one of their floundering operations.

"Miser," Benny yelled. He popped out of the seat at his console and sprinted to Miser's cubicle.

"What's up, boss?"

Benny leaned over the man's shoulder and motioned with his finger. "Get Katie's sector on the monitor."

Miser hit the keys.

Benny glanced toward the Kid's booth. "Kid, set up a track on this so we can document it."

"Got it, boss."

"Good," Benny said. "Now, you see that animal control truck? He just picked up a vicious dog, and he's gonna go right past Katie's house. With all those media trucks on the road, he'll probably swing into the other lane to avoid them. Katie's dog is alone in the yard. See him out there?"

Miser switched screens. "There he is."

"If we can get that bad dog out of that truck—"

"Sure thing, boss," Miser said. "If we just had another vehicle we could use," he called up another screen, "like that one right there, comin' down the highway. And, if we could get the two of them together on that ice somehow—"

"Distract him," Benny said.

"You got it. We'll just put that cigarette he's smokin' to work for us," Miser said. "Now, if we can get him sideways, about the time that car gets there, we might have something. See that curve," his finger touched the screen, "it's iced over. Watch this." Miser thumped his monitor screen.

Howard Mobley was on his last run of the day. He would deliver this troublesome dog to the kennel and then spend a raucous evening with his grandchildren.

Even though the Christmas fireworks he had picked up earlier in the day wouldn't be a surprise, they would be a big hit with the kids. A rosy Santa Claus grin formed on his cherubic face. He'd get a kick out of them, too.

He always did it the same way every year, just like his grandfather had done for him. He'd buy the fireworks, put them in individual brown paper bags, tie them with a simple piece of string, and write a kid's name on each bag. The best part would be when he drove into the driveway at the annual Christmas gathering. All the kids would drop whatever they were doing and charge the truck, leaping, and shouting, "Grandpa! Uncle Howard!" And for the next few hours, Uncle Howard would become the kid he used to be.

With those joyful thoughts in mind, he hadn't noticed the icy buildup in the curve he was now in until it was too late, and he found himself correcting for the skid. He had also forgotten the cigarette in his mouth, and when he cursed at his situation while he fought the wheel, it fell into his lap.

He quickly glanced down, spread his legs, raised up off the seat, swatted at the embers. By the time he heard the sound, he was in the other lane and facing an oncoming car, its horn blaring into his ears.

He cut the wheel.

The rear end of the truck skidded out of the turn and into the ditch on his right.

It struck the bank with a thud. He corrected for the skid, and the truck leaped back onto the highway.

The latch on the cage that held the dog he'd just picked up gave way under the twisting impact of the crash, and the dog leaped to freedom.

Howard Mobley hit the brake.

"Good job, Miser!" Benny straightened up. "There goes our killer dog. Now, let's see if he can find our little Freebie. Speaking of Freebie, where is he?"

The instant he said it, he realized that Freebie had vanished from the yard, and Katie was emerging from the kitchen door. Benny watched, transfixed, while Katie started down the steps on her way, he knew, to talk to the snowman.

Katie came out of the house and slowly climbed down the steps. A heavy coat and hood shielded her from the cold, and she held a tissue to her face. Her mother was taking her to the doctor this morning to find out why she was sick, but Mr. Devil was sick, too, and she wanted to see how he was doing before she left the house.

She stopped in front of the snowman. "Good morning, Mr. Devil." When the snowman didn't speak she continued. "I hope you're feeling better today. I don't feel so good," she said. "I must have caught what you've got. Mom is taking me to the doctor this morning and...."

"No, Katie. Go back in the house," Benny said with a calm, icy voice. "Go back in the house, sweetheart."

From around the far corner of the house, a black shape appeared in the back yard.

Benny nudged Miser's shoulder. "Stop the dog."

"Too late," Miser snapped. "He's got her spotted."

Freebie was nowhere in sight.

Its eyes now locked onto Katie, the dog ran directly at her.

Katie was talking to the snowman.

"No, Katie! Get out of there!"

Benny grabbed Miser by the collar and shook him viciously. "Stop the damn dog, Miser!"

"No time! There's no time!" Miser cried, his fingers hammering the keys.

"No, Katie! Run! Run! Somebody get her out of there!"

The dog closed on her. Rear legs driving it through the snow, its forelimbs leaving the ground, its back arching upward, teeth emerging from a black mouth, it leaped.

"No, Katie, *No!*"

While Benny watched helplessly, the scene unfolded on the screen in horrific slow motion. The dog sailed through the air in a perfect arc that would take it to Katie's throat. She was looking up, her attention trained on the snowman, when she suddenly caught a glimpse of the dog in her peripheral vision. The flash of terror in her eyes froze Benny's soul. Recognition was upon her, arms coming up, mouth beginning to open, he knew, to allow the scream to escape, her eyes beginning to close, the deadly teeth just inches away, when something emerged from the right side of the frame.

Freebie.

Stretched into a guided missile from nowhere, mouth gaping, every hair on his lean body a porcupine quill, Freebie collided with the other dog, burying his teeth into its thick neck.

Katie screamed and stumbled backwards.

Freebie's impact with the dog deflected its trajectory. They brushed past Katie and tumbled in the snow beyond her.

Armed only with tenacity and rage, Freebie

was no match for the larger animal. He fought gallantly, until the powerful jaws clamped down on his flanks.

The dogcatcher's truck skidded to a stop. He jumped from the cab and ran to the back just in time to see the dog he had captured tearing through Katie's snow-covered yard.

Had it not been for the snarling and the instantaneous scream, he might have let the dog go and concerned himself with the truck. However, the dog was his responsibility. If it injured or killed someone, especially during Christmas, he would never get over it.

Howard Mobley snatched open the passenger's door of his truck and grabbed his 357 Python from the glove box.

Katie's mother and father ran through the back door and into the yard, frantically shouting and waving their arms.

Mobley rounded the corner of the house, charging through the snow with the gun in his hand.

They converged on the girl.

The dogcatcher didn't see any blood on the girl, but she was screaming, and he couldn't take any chances. The dog was slinging around what was left of a smaller animal when he raised the pistol and fired.

Both animals fell limp into the bloody snow.

The gunfire had drawn the Atlanta police officers from the warmth of their cruisers and sent them sprinting across the yard.

Until now, the news crews had remained beyond the invisible property line, only for fear of being arrested for trespassing. Now the chaos in the yard sent them scurrying for position at the long driveway. They were ready when a car came roaring from behind the house and hurtled toward them with its lights on and its flashers pulsing.

"She's in there," someone yelled from the crowd as the car zipped past. "Katie Hart is in that car! Let's go!"

Madness ensued. Reporters and camera operators piled into their vehicles and roared after the Hart car as it sped away from them.

The convoy lurched into the parking lot of the Atlanta Animal Clinic.

Reporters leaped from their vehicles.

Rachael Hart struggled out of the car and rushed toward the vet's office with a bloody bundle in her arms. Katie and her father followed.

"...don't know what's going on," the GNG reporter said over his shoulder as he ran ahead of the camera that chased the action. "We heard a child scream, and then gunshots. We initially thought little Katie Hart had been attacked by the dog, but as you can see, she appears to be all right."

"Excuse me, sir. *Sir*? Can you tell us what happened?" He tried to head off the father at the door, but Hart pulled Katie ahead of him and dashed past the camera and into the clinic.

Dr. Thompson met them in the front office. He took the bundle from Rachael's arms and rushed into one of the examination rooms. Katie's father followed him through the door.

Rachael held her daughter and stroked her hair. "Now, now, it's going to be all right," she said. "Dr. Thompson will do everything he can do to help Freebie, darling."

"Is he hurt real bad, Mom?" Katie asked through her tears.

Katie's mother wiped her eyes. "Well, we don't know yet. We just have to wait and see what Dr. Thompson says after he's had a chance to examine him."

She placed a hand on Katie's face. "My goodness, child, you're burning up!" She guided Katie to a row of chairs where they sat and held each other. "That's all right. We'll get you to the doctor's office just as soon as we find out how

Freebie is doing. Can you tell me what's wrong?"

Katie shook her head. "I just feel bad all over."

"Maybe it's the flu," her mother said.

Katie shook her head, her face flushed and splotchy with fever. "I think I caught something from Mr. Devil. He's sick, too," she said.

Her mother squeezed her. "Oh, Katie, darling. I do wish you'd stop talking about the Devil. Christmas is coming and we have so many wonderful things to think about. You haven't talked about Santa Claus at all."

Paul Hart entered the room. Katie and her mother met him. He squatted down in front of Katie and held her hands.

When he didn't speak she said, "Freebie's hurt real bad isn't he, Daddy?"

His mouth quivering, her father nodded and swallowed hard. "Yes, he is, sweetheart, but Dr. Thompson is going to do everything he can do to save him for you. I told him...Freebie was...very special to you, and that we don't care how much it costs to save him. We'll just have to wait and see how it goes."

Katie wiped away her tears and said, "Thank you, Daddy. I love you." Then she collapsed on the floor.

...to a live report from the Georgia hospital where Joe Hendrick is standing by with the latest on little Katie Hart, who was admitted there this morning. Joe?

"Good evening, Richard. I'm standing in the shuttle corridor between the trauma wing and the main hospital at the Fosnes Medical Center in Atlanta, Georgia, where Katie Hart was brought this morning after she collapsed at a local veterinarian's office.

"If you recall, this is the eight-year-old girl who has charmed the world with her devilish Web site and her campaign to end Evil by praying for the Devil's redemption.

"We were outside her home this morning, when her family rushed her little dog to the vet's office after it was attacked by another dog. It initially was thought that Katie had been mauled in the attack, but that doesn't appear to be the case. We followed them to the vet's office, where ten minutes later Katie's father emerged from the building, his little girl limp in his arms, and rushed her here to the medical center. At this hour, we have no word on her condition.

"We have not been allowed inside with our cameras, however we do know that," he consulted his notes, "Dr. James Fosnes, Chief of Medical Staff at Fosnes Medical Center, is attending her. We also know that Dr. Jonathan Krueger, director of the prestigious immunology clinic named in his honor, and his team of internationally recognized immunologists, arrived just a few hours ago. We don't know the nature of the little girl's illness or her condition at this time, but apparently the situation is serious enough that the medical center has called in its big guns for this young lady. Richard?"

Joe, do we know why she collapsed?

"No, Richard. Apparently, the child was in perfect health—or so it was thought—until yesterday. Now she is suddenly the center of attention at this elite hospital.

"It's unfortunate as well, Richard, that her little dog—I think his name is Freebie—lies close to death at the vet's office. Katie was in her backyard this morning when a dog that had escaped from an animal control vehicle that skidded into a ditch threatened her. The larger dog apparently mauled Freebie when he attacked it in an attempt to protect Katie from harm.

"We will remain—"

"Here he comes! Here comes Fosnes!"

"Wait a minute, Richard. It appears," he was moving to his right, "that Dr. Fosnes is," now he was running with other reporters and news crews, the frame leaping about as the videographer and the audio technician ran behind him, "out of the building. Dr. Fosnes? Excuse me, doctor. Could we have a word with you? How is Katie Hart?

What can you tell us about her condition? Is she conscious?"

The reporter finally cut him off. "Doctor, I'm sure you're aware of who she is, and that millions of people out there would like to know what's wrong with their angel. What can you tell us about Katie Hart's condition?"

Fosnes finally stopped. A swarm of reporters and camera support personnel collided with one another as they surrounded him. The strain in his face was apparent as he spoke.

"We have not arrived at a diagnosis. I'd like to say we have her stabilized, but I cannot say that, either. She's awake, but her vital signs continue to fail. She has an extremely high fever, but there is no sign of a viral infection, bacterial agents, poisons, or trauma. It would appear that her immune system has failed, and her body is attacking itself. However, we have no evidence of problematic antigens, and consequently, no buildup of antibodies to support that theory. It's a puzzle. Dr. Krueger, director of the Krueger Institute, and his team of immunologists are with her now. It's a waiting game."

"So you don't know what's wrong with her?"

Fosnes hesitated. "That's correct."

"Doctor, do you think this has anything to do with the Devil?"

"I'm a doctor, not a minister. I don't—"

"*I'm* a minister, and yes it does."

The cameras swung in the direction of the outburst.

"And who are you, sir?" Joe asked.

"My name is Reverend Fred Frey, and I have every reason to believe this is the work of Satan."

"So you believe Satan made Katie sick?"

"Yes," Frey said. "I'm convinced of it." He noticed the GNG logo on the videographer's jacket and the live-feed trucks looming in the plaza area beyond the cameras. He knew his words would go worldwide as soon as they left his mouth. Although he didn't know why Satan would destroy this child when she was playing into his hands, this was his chance to right a terrible wrong.

"This is Katie's reward for attempting to be Satan's friend," he said, "and this is his response to her actions. Let this be a warning to all those who would align themselves with the Beast. I call upon the people of the world to pray for little Katie Hart, and for the ones who have followed her example, to give up this senseless and destructive preoccupation with saving the Devil!"

With her husband by her side, Katie's mother methodically stroked her daughter's hair with a brush and spoke tenderly. "We'll know something by tomorrow, darling. All the test results will be back by morning, and the doctors will know what's wrong. Then they can make you well."

Katie slowly rolled her head toward her mother. "I'm going to die, Mom."

Her mother laid down the brush and squeezed her daughter's hand. "Oh, darling, you're not going to die," she said, rubbing the hand. She kissed Katie. "You're going to get well and be home tomorrow so you can open all those presents Santa Claus is going to leave under your tree."

Katie shook her head. "The doctors don't know what's wrong with me. They didn't believe me when I told them that I caught whatever Mr. Devil has. He was very sick the last time he came to see me. I haven't seen him since then. I hope he doesn't die, too," she said.

Her mother hugged her.

"Mom? Is Freebie okay?"

Paul Hart laid his hand on his wife's arm.

"He's doing great, darling," her mother said and started to cry. "Dr. Thompson is taking good care of him. I'm sure he'll be home by Christmas, too."

"I'd like to see him," Katie said.

"I don't think the hospital will let us bring him in here, sweetheart," her father said.

Katie reached for her father's hand. "Please bring him to me, Dad. I want to see my Freebie before I die."

Sam Boyle entered Michael Stoecker's office at WayCoolKids headquarters without knocking and stopped in front of the desk. The sun had already plunged below the horizon behind the extinct volcanoes and left a fiery magenta sky in its wake. He pitched a fistful of papers onto the desktop. He did not sit. "Rush-hour might be over. Traffic on her site is slowing down. You see the little speech that preacher gave?"

Stoecker had his television tuned to the GNG live coverage of Katie Hart's story from the Fosnes Medical Center in Atlanta. "Yes. And her doctors still don't know what's wrong with her. According to GNG sources on the scene they don't expect her to live much longer."

"From the looks of these," Boyle pointed to the papers, "her movement appears to be dying with her. You're looking at a small sample of her q-mails that support the declining numbers."

Q-mail was company jargon representing "questionable mail." WayCoolKids purposely scanned all e-mail messages and Web site content on their site for hundreds of words—q-words—considered inappropriate for their young clients. Even though client confidentially was priority number two at WayCoolKids, the company systematically searched e-mail containing q-words for anything that would possibly offend, abuse or pose a threat to any child who used their service. They analyzed suspicious e-mail and labeled it q-mail. All q-mail warranting investigation was reported to the proper authorities. WayCoolKids's contract clearly stated the company's rigid policy of e-mail monitoring and client protection—priority number one—and left no question that it would be strictly enforced. Such restrictive guidelines inevitably produced borderline e-mail messages that would be read, considered, then released to the intended recipient. The e-mails on Stoecker's desk fit that category.

"These people are all mad at the Devil and won't be praying for his salvation any longer," Boyle said. "Based on the q-mails we've isolated and the declining number of hits on her site, I'd say there are many thousands of e-mails going to her box that support this trend."

Stoecker turned his chair to face the dying western sky with his fingers propped in thought. "Hellish sunset," he said.

"Hellish situation, too," Boyle added.

"Yes. Put an interactive alert screen on her site. We'll use it to keep people who go to her Web page informed about her progress. It's the least we can do."

Benny entered the Devil's lair and sauntered to the coffee table with his hands carelessly shoved into his pockets. Satan rested comfortably in the old recliner, a cigar sticking out of his mouth, ignoring Benny. Gone was the old man who was close to something resembling death just two days ago. Buffalo roamed across the large screen embedded in The Wall.

Benny noted the orange flicker of the Overlook—now at its full brilliance once again—and said, "It's the prayer thing isn't it?" He nodded confirmation of that thought when Satan didn't speak, still avoiding eye contact with him. "Yeah, that's it," he affirmed. "It's been the prayer thing all along."

He began to pace an imaginary courtroom. "It *does* something to you, something...bad, something *so bad* that stopping it is worth killing an innocent little child who loves you."

Satan silently chewed the cigar.

"Why didn't I see it before now?" Benny continued. He shook his head and paced. "Katie starts praying for you. You get all hot under the collar. She keeps praying, and you mount this all-out campaign to stop her—at a time when we're already overrun with critically important operations. She keeps praying, you start using the remote to control your operations screens, and then," he stopped pacing, spun around, and pointed a finger at Satan, "you get sick." He paced again. "Then, more people pray for you, your signal gets weak, you lose control of all your operations, the more people who pray for you the sicker you get, and then two days ago, you're comatose.

"Now look at you," Benny said. "The epitome of health and fitness. And my little Katie? She's dying...."

"Sit down, Benny," Satan said quietly.

"You lousy bastard!"

Benny's words reverberated off the stone walls. Satan didn't flinch. He removed the cigar from his mouth. "It's done, Benny. Sit down. Let's talk about it."

"Maybe I don't wanna sit down!" Benny yelled. "Maybe I've been sittin' down long enough! I don't take orders from you anymore! And talk about what? Just like you said, it's done. There's nothing left to talk about!"

"That's right," Satan exploded. He sprang out of the chair. "It's all been said. I talked...and I talked...and I *talked*. I gave her every chance I could give her," he raged. "*Every chance*!" He stuck his finger in Benny's face, "And, she *still* continues to defy me!

"And yes, prayin' for me makes me powerless, strips away my evil armor, allows...love to enter my heart, like it has for this little girl! So, now you know the Devil's only weakness! Satan's," he waved his hand about, "*fatal flaw*!

"So what am I supposed to do, just give up everything I have ever worked for? Give up the one thing that I can call my own? Don't you understand?" His fingers pounded his chest. "I...am...*Satan*! I have an empire at stake here!"

"An *empire*?" Benny thundered. "You stupid old fool! All you've got's an overrated barbecue pit and a bunch of worthless losers who wouldn't spit on you if you caught on fire!"

"Just like you, I guess!"

"Yeah, that's right, old man," Benny shouted in his face, "just like me!"

"Enough, Counselor!"

Satan grabbed Benny by the collar and hurled him through the virtual glass of the Overlook and into the fires of Hell.

15

December 24, Christmas Eve

Thousands had gathered in the plaza and surrounding areas on this frozen Christmas Eve. The Fosnes Medical Center and every building in sight floated in a flickering sea of fire and crystallized breath that grew larger by the amber glow of each candle that flared to life.

Made possible by GNG's new Remote Audiovisual Satellite Interface system, the company had cancelled most of its scheduled programming on this evening and geared up to cover Katie's story. Requiring no video or audio cable runs, the multi-camera RASI system went up in hours instead of days.

Television lights erected on short notice clung to portable towers that reached into the night. A single podium, impaled with microphones, standing silent and forlorn in the glare outside the towering glass entryway of the medical center, awaited the harbingers who would eventually appear and notify a hopeful world of little Katie Hart's fate.

Local family and friends had been called in. Reverend Frey had held a prayer meeting with them in the ICU waiting room. The doctors had told the parents that modern medicine could not save Katie, and that she was possibly just minutes away from death. The doctors and everyone except immediate family had been asked to wait in the chapel until it was over. Now Reverend Frey held one of Katie's hands. Her mother held the other one.

Katie's father entered the room and approached the bed with a bundle in his arms. "Look who's here," he said. He carefully laid it in the crook of Katie's arm and unfolded the blanket.

Katie slowly tipped her head sideways. "Freebie?" she managed to say. She gazed up at her father with tears in her distant eyes. "Is this my Freebie?"

"Yes, sweetheart," her father said tenderly, "it's Freebie. We didn't want you to see him like this."

"Is he going to die, too?"

Freebie slowly and painfully raised his head

and moaned at the sound of Katie's voice.

Her father wept. "Yes, sweetheart. He's going to live with Jesus, too. You'll both go to Heaven together...."

Reverend Frey laid his hands on Katie's arm. "Our Father in Heaven, though sorrow blinds our eyes to the good in this act, we take comfort in the fact that your mighty hand moves upon us this eve of our Savior's birth, that we are not alone, that your merciful love surrounds us.

"The world awaits your judgement, precious Lord. If it be your will, oh mighty God, we pray that you bless this family with guidance and insight. Deliver them from the pain of uncertainty in this dark hour, that they and the rest of the world may see the wisdom in your actions.

"Father in Heaven, omniscient and loving God, creator, giver, and taker, of all life, we pray that you bless this precious child and receive her into your arms, as you did your own Son in his final hour on this earth, that she may walk the streets of Heaven, hand-in-hand with Jesus Christ our Lord and Savior, with little Freebie by her side.

"Oh, merciful Lord, give us a reason to rejoice, for we are truly hurt, lost, and in desperate need of your eternal blessing. All this we pray in the name of Jesus. Amen."

"And please," Katie whispered. "Mr. Devil has been sick, too, and I pray that he gets well very soon. God bless Mr. Devil."

Katie closed her eyes and drifted into eternity.

Freebie expelled a sharp breath and a yelp before his head fell onto her arm.

"Don't do it, Katie. Please don't do it!" Satan cried.

...well very soon. God bless Mr. Devil—

"No, no...*Noooooo!*"

Satan killed the big screen.

He viciously hurled the remote against the Overlook glass then grabbed his head and stumbled through the room, wailing in deep, wretched shrieks of agony that shook the foundations of Hell.

What had he done? In order to save an empire that meant nothing to him, he had destroyed a helpless child who had the courage to love him. In doing so, he had created a new demon, a demon even more wicked than himself. What had he done?

He staggered to a stop and transformed into the Beast. It threw its head back, and a grievous roar burst from its throat.

Unable to withstand the concussion, the virtual glass that enclosed the Overlook shattered.

A firestorm burst out of the depths of Hell and into the room, transforming the chamber into an inferno. Flames poured over the lip of the

Overlook and spilled across the floor like molten lava.

The monster stood motionless in a shallow lake of bubbling fire, its arms limp, shoulders slumped. It took one awkward step, then another, and another, until it stopped at the coffee table, where the red phone, the hotline to God, waited in silence.

It stared down at the phone, then careened its head upward and spewed a fountain of flames from its mouth. It dropped to its knees and broke down into pitiful, moaning sobs. Slowly, with ancient hands, it brushed away the cobwebs that entombed the phone, picked up the receiver, and dialed with the pointed fingernail on its left forefinger.

Dr. Fosnes emerged from the medical center followed by an entourage of other doctors and approached the podium. He appeared ghost-like in his long white coat under the harsh television lights. Layers of reporters and photographers crouched below the video cameras in the front row of the crowd.

"My name is Dr. James Fosnes, Chief of Medical Staff at Fosnes Medical Center." He checked his watch and sighed. "At approximately 9:41 p.m., Eastern Standard Time, a little over twenty minutes ago, Ms. Katie Lynn Hart expired from—"

The massive crowd issued a gasp.

"—from causes we don't fully understand," Fosnes went on.

Murmurs rose from the crowd.

"She was admitted to the medical center yesterday in a state of semi-consciousness, and tests revealed an extensive and rapidly progressing degeneration of her immune system. As I stated yesterday, it appears that her immune system was attacking her body. All the tests we performed returned negative results, meaning we didn't find any abnormalities that would indicate failure of the immune system or any other natural functions. It appears that Miss Hart simply...expired.

"The family sends their deepest appreciation to everyone who has supported Katie. They remain with her now, and ask that you please understand the pain they feel, which is why they choose not to face the cameras at this time."

"What killed her, doctor?" a reporter asked.

"As I said before, her immune system failed. At this time we do not have a medical explanation as to *why* it failed."

Satan killed her! That's why it failed!

The allegation surfaced from deep within the throng, a lone, agonized cry filled with emotion and rage.

For a moment, Fosnes stared blankly into the lights. The past several hours of his attempt to save Katie Hart flashed before him in vivid detail. The team had exhausted the culmination of their experience and technology, along with the vast resources of their worldwide medical research and conferencing network, and still didn't have an answer. As difficult as it was to accept, there was no medical explanation for the child's death. The words of Reverend Fred Frey reverberated in his head: *The modern medicine of man has no power over Satan's wrath.*

Within the millisecond it took for Fosnes to frame a response to the pseudo-prophet's accusation, the words rose out of the fiery sea and into an emotional tidal wave that swept into the microphones and across the world landscape.

Sam Boyle sat stunned in front of his console and digested the doctor's words. Just eleven days ago, this perfectly healthy little girl had put her message to encourage people to pray for the Devil on her Web site, and now she was dead.

He punched up Katie's Web page. The interactive alert screen glared at him, defying him to do what he must. His phone rang and spared him momentarily.

It was Michael Stoecker. "Yes. I saw it," Boyle said with a great sigh. No, he didn't believe it either. No, he hadn't posted the message.... Yes, he would post it, burn the CDs, and archive the site for historical purposes.

He hung up.

Archive the site. Burn the CDs. Delay the closure.

For the next five minutes, he set up the backup and waited while the massive database transferred the contents of folder KH#8904-783 to the high-speed tape backup. He removed the three tapes from the backup drive and stacked them on his console bench. One would go to Records, one to Michael Stoecker's desk, and one would go to an off-site data repository where it would live behind locked steel doors. He was certain the CDs were for the family. If requested, they would be mailed, a complete volume of all e-mail transcripts from Katie's site. Going through them would be a terrible ordeal for the parents; over four hundred million messages were on record....

Anyway, not his problem. Stoecker's job was to handle the dirty work; his job was to burn a copy of the file onto CDs. That took another fifteen minutes while he went for a drink of water, to the bathroom, anything to keep from watching a child's impossible dream become nothing more than a footnote in history.

When he returned, he labeled the CDs, laid them aside, punched up the interactive alert screen on Katie's Web page. What to write...? Date? Time? Legal format? Abbreviated format? The message. *We regret to inform you....* Too formal. Maybe he should just repeat the doctor's words. Yeah, that's it, take the easy way out. Sam Boyle never took the easy way out. At least he could be creative.

But Sam Boyle was angry, and he didn't feel like being creative. He felt like being blunt. He felt like someone had stolen something from him, robbed him and the world of a treasure, and he felt like making sure everyone else in the world knew it. So he put his hands on the keys and wrote what he felt.

KATIE HART IS DEAD....

The confirmation screen appeared, and he held the Mouse pointer over the OK control button for the longest time before he clicked. He watched the message appear in the interactive alert screen. He would leave it there until tomorrow morning when he disabled Katie Hart's Web page.

He collected the backups and the CDs, killed the lights in his cubicle, and left the screen up for anyone to see. He would drop off the CDs at Michael's office and go home.

Thirty minutes had elapsed since Stoecker had called. When the door to the engineering section of WayCoolKids Inc. closed behind Sam Boyle, a deathly quiet settled over the shadowy room. Only the muffled whir of computer white noise remained behind to witness the event. Without warning, the last word in the message inside the interactive alert screen on Katie Hart's Web page changed from "DEAD...." to "ALIVE!", and the message began to flash.

KATIE HART IS ALIVE!
KATIE HART IS ALIVE!

Reporters hovered like vultures over a kill at the entrance to the west wing corridor that led to Katie's room. City police officers and the threat of arrest prevented them from entering the desolate hallway where they waited for a glimpse of the parents.

Within minutes of the death, the parents and their minister had retired to the chapel where they prayed and waited for nurses to clear the room of the medical technology that could not save Katie. They had not returned, and only doctors, staff, and people who could justify their presence with a family member admitted to this floor were allowed to pass through the barricade.

"Excuse me." Dressed as a doctor, Satan approached from behind the mob and spoke softly, stethoscope around his neck, Santa Claus hat on his head, hands resting casually in his white coat pockets. He politely slipped between reporters and crewmembers with a pleasant smile and a "thank you" when someone moved aside. "Excuse me, please...thank you...thank you." He acknowledged the police officers with, "Good evening, gentlemen. Thank you for your support." Without breaking his stride, he spoke to the occasional nurse as he proceeded down the stark white hallway. "Good evening." If the family were in the room, they'd be too grief-stricken to question him. "Merry Christmas." If nurses were in the room, he'd exercise authority over them and send them away so he could...be with the family. "Good evening. Merry Christmas." If doctors were there...then, so be it. He'd do what he must.

When he arrived at room 564, he swung the door open and swept into the room.

She was alone.

It was a small private room, pink, one bed, blinds closed, two sleeper recliners and three folding chairs hastily arranged to accommodate family and friends, flowers everywhere a place could be found to put them, shadowy, deathly quiet.

He approached the bed and laid his hands on the rails. The tubes and support machinery had been disconnected and removed from the room—less painful for the family. Her face wasn't covered. Her eyes were closed, and her hair had been brushed. Her little dog still lay in the cradle of her arm. Early Christmas presents surrounded her. Colorful bows and the remains of wrapping paper littered the foot of the bed. He read one of the tags: *To Katie, from Santa.* He glanced at the others, all from Santa.

She was beautiful, even in death. He picked up her hand and held it in his, leaning on the bed rail, and smiled. "Merry Christmas, my Angel. It's all over."

He gently stroked Freebie's head. "Good dog."

Voices. Weeping. The family was returning to the room.

He pressed her hand to his cheek then kissed it, God's power manifesting itself within him as he did so. "God bless you, Katie. I love you, sweetheart."

Katie's father and Reverend Frey pushed through the door with Katie's mother at the point of collapse pressed between them, the father sobbing, Reverend Frey calling on his God.

"...us, Lord! Help us find a way to—"

"Why did my baby have to die? I just don't understand why my baby had to die!" Rachael Hart cried out.

They struggled to get her to a chair where the father held her and they wept together.

Reverend Frey dropped to his knees beside

them and held Rachael's hand to his forehead. "Oh merciful God! Lay your mighty hand on this family and ease their pain! Come into this room and comfort these tortured souls! Show us a sign!"

"Why do you weep, when there is cause for great celebration?"

They discovered the doctor. He stood facing them, next to Katie's bed, her hand held in his.

Reverend Frey shot up from the floor. "In God's name, man, what is the meaning of this? This family's child just died!"

The doctor smiled. "But there must be some mistake." He glanced back at Katie. "This child *lives*, and so does her dog." He laid Katie's hand on Freebie.

The dog moaned.

"What?" Reverend Frey said, gaining control of his senses. "Who are you, and what are you doing in this room?"

The doctor presented his ID that hung from the lapel of his white coat and shook the Reverend's hand. "I'm sorry. I'm Doctor Deville, and Katie is my friend. You must be Reverend Frey."

The doctor instantly transformed into the demon that was Satan, and just as quickly, back into the doctor while still holding Reverend Frey's hand.

"Hello, Fred. Merry Christmas, and God bless you."

Reverend Frey's eyes flew wide with shock. "Satan!"

The preacher passed out and collapsed on the floor.

Satan walked to the door then stopped and looked back at the stunned parents. "God sends his blessing. Merry Christmas."

The last thing he heard as he entered the hallway was "Mommy, is that you?"

He smiled. "Thank you, Lord."

"Oh, my God! Oh, my God!" Katie's mother yelled.

"Mommy?"

The parents rushed to the bed.

"Katie! Oh, Katie! My precious baby!"

Katie opened her eyes.

Her mother held her face and kissed her. "Oh, my God! You're alive!" She scrambled for the nurse's call button and held it down. "Someone please get a doctor in here! Please hurry!"

"That was him, Mom," Katie murmured while her mother and father lavished attention on her.

"Who, darling?" her mother asked.

"That doctor," Katie said. "That was Mr. Devil. He came to help me. I knew he would. I just knew it."

Katie heard a soft whine.
Freebie opened his eyes and licked her arm.

16

Deep within the bowels of Hell, a grotesque figure, singing *Frosty the Snowman*, shuffled its way down a scabrous tunnel. The demon's shadow flashed from wall to wall as it passed openings where the flare of Hell's fire belched into its path.

The tunnel opened into a sprawling expanse of hellish, boiling red light—the Lake of Fire. Licking flames curled from its endless, eternal surface. Still singing about Frosty, the demon shuffled on from the shore, out across the lake, and faded into the fiery distance.

Direction wasn't a problem in this evil dimension. The Beast knew the location of every soul that floated in the fire, like stars in the night sky. That would soon change, for there would be no souls here. When it arrived at its destination, it grunted a sigh of relief. Benny Hart's soul dangled in the flames, suspended in a delicate tormenting balance between existence and oblivion designed to inflict the ultimate punishment called Hell.

The demon slowly eased Benny's limp form down and draped it across its shoulder. "Merry Christmas, Benny," it said. The demon changed its song to *Deck the Halls* and retraced its steps back through the flames.

Satan entered the crew's sleeping crypt, a stark, utilitarian vault where bodies floated within it on individual beds of eternal flame. The subtle white noise of Hell's distant roar pushed through flame jets in the floor.

He gently laid Benny on one of the flaming beds.

He moved on and knelt next to Bleeder. Bleeder's chest rose and settled peacefully in stark contrast to the haunted mind that lurked underneath the blanket of sleep.

Satan laid his hand on Bleeder's head. "Do not awaken, Bleeder," he whispered.

Bleeder squirmed, then breathed deep, exhaled, and slipped back into his nightmares.

"That's right," Satan said, "go back to sleep.

Everything's gonna be all right. We're gonna have a party later, and tomorrow will be a new day, and by the grace of God, you will no longer live in torment."

He moved on to the Miser. Miser lay curled into a fetal position, yelping quietly instead of snoring. Satan smiled compassionately. "And what are we gonna do for you, Miser? You know, I think we might try to find you and me a nice dog...."

The scene outside the Fosnes Medical Center had gone from a crowd of the faithful, to a churning sea of protesters shouting anti-Satan slogans, to what could only be called a prayer vigil fit for a saint. Flowing out of delivery vans that couldn't get near the building, streams of flowers continued to meander through the crowd on their way to the entrance of the medical center. The muted sound of weeping and prayers hovered in the frosty night air. Thousands of candle flames glowed in the white mist, amber glimmers of hope that began to fade with the resolve of their bearers. Katie Hart was dead, and nothing would bring her back.

Having delivered the news of Katie's death, Fosnes and his staff had returned to the medical center. The hospital chaplain had replaced them at the podium in an attempt to offer some semblance of closure for the lingering mass of people on this most holy night. GNG's cameras were still sending the event to the world; however, the buzz on the headsets was that preparations were being made to "wrap it up." The chaplain was praying now, the final act in his message to a world that mourned the death of this innocent crusader. "And as we go from this place of great sorrow tonight, let us set our own lives in order. Let us find comfort in the fact that long ago our Savior, Jesus Christ, was born on Christmas day, that even in death we might live forever in His presence."

The double glass doors of the medical center suddenly sprang open and a man bounded past them.

"...commend the soul of Miss Katie Lynn Hart into His hands, so that in the words of Jesus himself, where He is there she may be also. Amen."

The man leaped onto the podium as the chaplain backed away from the microphones.

Their eyes met. It was—or what seemed to be left of—the Reverend Fred Frey. His shirt was unbuttoned and rumpled. His tie hung around his neck like a lasso. His hair resembled a clump of sagebrush in a heavy wind. And his eyes were electric, ablaze with wonder. "Are you all right, Reverend?"

The words went into the microphones, and the interruption drew murmurs from the crowd.

Fred didn't speak to the chaplain. He just shouted into the microphones. "Praise Jesus, hallelujah!"

His fist struck the podium. "I said, all you people on the hill back there! I wanna hear it from everybody! Our precious Lord and Savior, Jesus Christ, walks among us on this eve of his birth! Katie Hart is *alive!"*

Frey's words snuffed out the dismal mood that held the earth in its grip, and ignited a blaze of worldwide jubilation.

Praise Jesus, hallelujah!

Fred grabbed the chaplain and crushed the man in a bear hug.

Pandemonium swept through the mass of people.

Anticipating the crowd roar that followed, GNG's location director called for camera one, the locked down wide shot of the Fosnes Medical Center complex that revealed the immense scale of the event. "Open mikes, let the good times roll, people. Ready camera four on the podium. We'll take it on the lull if we ever get one. Standby, two. Here we go."

Camera operators on the towers, lighting technicians—GNG's entire location crew—threw themselves into the air.

"Praise Jesus, hallelujah!" Satan shouted.

His control room staff shoved their fists into the air and cheered. "Praise Jesus, hallelujah!"

They all stood around him in his main chamber, Christmas decorations draped across their arms and around their necks, Santa Claus hats on all their heads, big Havana cigars sticking through their teeth, watching the action on the large operations screen.

Satan milled about with a cigar in his mouth and his arm around Benny, slapping others on the back, shaking their hands, grabbing the tinsel off their arms and throwing it into the air.

After a few moments of unrestrained comradery, he called for quiet. He removed the cigar from his mouth and shoved the other hand into a pocket on the battered housecoat.

His crew shuffled into a small group, all grinning around their cigars.

Satan cleared his throat. When he spoke, he spoke quietly. "No doubt this comes as a surprise." He chuckled. "Who'd have ever thought the Devil would go straight?"

Tentative chuckles rose from the crew.

"Well," he said, "little Katie Hart did. You, the world, generations past, and generations to come all have her to thank for what has happened. Me? I'm just an old angel who, because of a child's courage, has finally learned to love again." He gave a little shrug and grunted. “With God, all things are possible. Right?”

Shouts of approval.

“Now,” he said briskly. “The details are still sketchy, but the concept is sound. This event will of course change the shape of the universe, but the fires of Hell will continue to burn, and from now on, they’ll be put to good use. With your help, we’re gonna do God’s work in a way never before possible.”

More cheers.

He put the cigar back in his mouth, then grinned. “Oh, and Benny, round up all of our air conditioning technicians and get them up here. We need to cool this place down.”

His crew cheered again, then hauled him up on their shoulders and danced around the room.

17

Christmas Day

Katie darted through the back door and down the steps to Snowman. "Good morning, Mr. Devil. I'm so happy to see you!"

"Good morning, Katie," Satan said.

"I just knew you'd help me get well." She lowered her head for a moment then said, "I know you made me sick. That's what everyone is saying. But I'm glad you changed your mind, and I forgive you.

"Freebie is fine. The doctor said we can bring him home in a day or two. Thank you for saving him, too.

"I have to go soon. I just wanted to come out and say goodbye. We're going to spend the day and night with Grandma. She lives a long way from here. I'm going to New York the next day to be on the Today show, so I won't see you for a while." She looked up at a bright blue sky. "The sun is out, and it's getting warmer." She paused and sniffled. "I'm going to miss Snowman. I don't suppose he'll be here when I get back."

Satan gave her a loving smile. "No, Katie," he said tenderly, "Snowman won't be here."

"Will you be here?"

Satan chuckled. "Yes, sweetheart, I'll always be here."

He stood in front of his operations screen dressed in brass-toed red cowboy boots, wooly white chaps, a red ranch shirt, a black and white vest with long, red-leather fringe across the front and back, and a black ten-gallon hat. He tugged at his belt like the boys out west do and said, "I'm gonna take a few days off, but I'll be back soon. Then we'll talk and talk and talk about everything that's happened."

"Oh good!" she said, "There's so much I want to know." She pressed her little hands together. "Well I have to go now. I hope you have a wonderful Christmas Day."

She ran back across the yard. After a short distance, she stopped and threw a kiss over her shoulder at Snowman, then yelled, "I love you!"

Satan wiped his eye.

A single tear cut a groove down Snowman's cheek.

"I love you too, Angel," Satan said as she disappeared into the house.

He reached inside the vest and pulled a small Christmas card from his shirt pocket. A snowman on the cover greeted him with a wave. He had little red horns drawn on his head. Once again Satan read the caption inside the card. *Merry Christmas*! *I love you! Katie*.

The scraggly, blinking Christmas tree in the corner next to the Overlook caught his attention, as did the room. Christmas decorations covered the walls. Big frosty snowflakes hung from the ceiling. Artificial snow drifted against and clung to the perimeter of the Overlook. The crew had done a good job.

Satan smiled warmly, pulled a cigar from a vest pocket and stuck it into his mouth, then switched on GNG with the remote. The news anchorman popped onto one of the five monitors below the main operations screen.

...to this special edition of GNG news. Good morning, I'm Richard Atworthy in Washington. Short of the actual birth of Jesus Christ some two

thousand years ago, this Christmas Day promises to be one of the most extraordinary moments in human history. Beginning with the death and miraculous recovery of little Katie Hart last night, international peacemaking, and several major worldwide humanitarian events dominate this morning's two-hour special report from GNG headquarters in Washington.

First, we take you to China where the Democratic Freedom Fighters liberation front has laid down its weapons and declared that it will disband. This comes just hours after the Chinese government stunned the world by announcing the political freedom of Taiwan and Tibet, the return of the Dalai Lama to his homeland, and that free elections will be held in China in the coming year. We have more on this remarkable development from—

Satan laughed. "Yeah, that's better." He repeatedly punched the remote, bringing up one news station after another on the remaining monitors.

...supported rebels are said to have pulled out of the Sudan and are refusing to fight any longer. The Libyan government gave no explanation for its actions, except to say they have had, quote, "a change of heart in the interests of humanity." We have more on this dramatic shift in Libyan policy from—

...us that political and military leaders in North Korea have agreed to offers of financial and

humanitarian aid in exchange for domestic freedom in that country. North Korea's military has pulled out of the demilitarized zone, and a North Korean delegation is being deployed to South Korea to establish a long-awaited dialogue between the two—

...killer virus in Africa has been isolated, and authorities from several nations are joining forces to contain this—

...reports coming in by the hour continue to document extraordinary events. This one just in, we have reports from several major cities in the United States that record numbers of criminals are turning themselves in to local authorities. Precincts in New York City and Washington, DC are being overrun—

...regional news this morning, city power officials in Chicago and other major cities throughout the United States are reporting a drastic cut in residential and commercial power usage. It seems that thermostats are being turned off. Lumadine, one of Chicago's most aggressive power consumers, reports that automatic thermal overrides shut down its heating units during the night. As one company official put it, "Heat appears to be coming out of the floor."

"Good, good! It's working!"

...forecasters say the record cold snap in the frigid southeastern United States has been broken

as the jet stream sweeps north, and warmer temperatures are in the forecast for—

...unprecedented events continue to pour into the GNG newsroom on this unusual Christmas morning. Churches and food banks are being inundated with food and donations. Some of the most notorious and violent gangs in America are reportedly banding together and volunteering their manpower to distribute food to the poor. The United Mission Alliance claims that thousands of homeless people are being offered places to live—

...police departments throughout the United States continue to report zero crime rates since midnight last night....

On the main screen, the sun hung large and warm in a cloudless morning sky above Snowman and Katie's backyard, its rays pushing showers of snow from the burdened trees. Tiny droplets of water found their way along whatever journey would take them to the thawing earth. Snowman stood alone and silent in his domain, his job now finished and his days numbered by events beyond his control. One of his arms was already beginning to droop, and his horns were melting.

Satan punched the remote.

A vast herd of buffalo appeared on the screen. They roamed an endless snowy plain painted with red-cliff escarpments and towering volcanic buttes surrounded by a brilliant blue sky.

Satan pitched the remote onto the couch and waved his big black hat above his head. He burst into a joyous laugh and cried, "Merry Christmas, everybody!"

While the good news reports continued to roll in on the monitors, he snapped his fingers, and a whirlwind of blue mist swept him up and into the wintry western panorama.